I0532923

Mystery, Malevolence & Murder
Collected Stories: Volume One

A Compilation by David T. Boyd

(Second Edition)

TM
Another Shore Press, LLC
www.anothershorepress.com

MYSTERY, MALEVOLENCE & MURDER
Collected Stories: Volume One

Edited by: Rolf Wolff
Cover Design by: David P. Schafer

Published by:
Another Shore Press, LLC
PO Box 381030
Brooklyn, New York 11238
www.anothershorepress.com

ISBN: 978-0-9832484-3-9

To Wayne Hugh Sick. You are loved and missed.

INTRODUCTION
***

As I began writing these short stories I'd already entertained the idea of developing a concept rather than slapping pages together and adding a title. Because of the success of *Falling Down*, plus the amount of readers who said they are anxiously awaiting the follow-up, titled *Ubiquity*, I'd decided to provide an introduction to one of the upcoming book's characters; a former homicide detective for the Chicago Police Department named Seth Aloysius Green, Jr. You may simply call him 'Al' for short.

Detective Green was with the CPD for twenty years, and though solving homicides was what he did for a living, his passion was writing. Upon his retirement he managed to publish his first mystery novel titled *A Late Frost*, which made the New York Times Best Seller List. Since then Al has been in high demand, going on to publish three subsequent novels with equal success, one of which is being developed into a screenplay for a feature film. Always being a person who believes in giving a helping hand, Al decided to post an announcement on his author website, www.detectivealgreen.com, for an annual short story writing contest titled "Mystery, Malevolence & Murder." The only guideline was the stories had to be set in major metropolitan areas. The top short stories that make the cut receive special acknowledgment on his website, in addition to being published in *Urban Mystery Archives,* a quarterly magazine that Al personally founded a few years ago.

As you read and learn more about Al, I'm sure you'll find him to be a likeable guy, but very no-nonsense, highly intelligent and knowledgeable on a vast array of subjects. Al is of African-American descent and grew up on Chicago's South Side where he's lived his entire life.

Enjoy the book, as I expect you'll like meeting Al as much as I enjoyed creating and writing about him.

Enjoy!
Dave

CONTEST FINALISTS
(Courtesy of Detective Al's Website)

Dear Mystery Enthusiasts:

It is with great pleasure that I announce the collected works from our first three annual *Mystery, Malevolence & Murder* short story contests. These stories were in previous editions of *The Urban Mystery Archives*, and due to popular demand, they are here in book format for the first time. They are as follows:

William Roberson - *"The Voice Within"*
Eve Adamsley - *"Nicholas"*
Arnold Jackson - *"Paranoia"*
Roberta Sanchez - *"Remembrance"*
Edward Urban - *"Always"*
Ursula Tompkins - *"Three On A Match"*
Bartholomew Palmer - *"The Peril of Rancor"*
Ingrid Davis - *"A Fan of Ms. 45"*
Quincy Powell - *"Ten Twenty-Four"*
Ulysses Candelario - *"Communiqué"*
Ina Austin - *"In Timely Fashion"*
Teresa Rodriguez - *"Sweet Serendipity"*
Yohann Sebastian - *"The Warden of Souls"*

I would like to thank all those who participated in this contest, and I'm very grateful to you for making my reading so interesting over the past few years. Please remember to periodically check my website, www.detectivealgreen.com, for the official announcement of future winners and look for more tales of suspense in upcoming editions of Urban Mystery Archives.

Thanks again for your participation, enjoy the stories and keep on writing!

Sincerely,
Seth Aloysius Green, Jr.
AKA - Detective Al

The Voice Within
By William Roberson
***

3:59am

"--on CBS AM Radio 1000 where you get the latest in news, sports and weather." CLICK!

Arthur Dean turned off his clock radio and sat on the right side of his king sized bed, his mind filled with the same dismal thoughts that haunted him day after day. He listened to his heart beating in the darkness. It was time to put an end to this nightmare, and he was ready. He glanced at the nightstand, noting the time.

4:00am

It was the middle of a breezy fall season in Chicago and day wouldn't break for a while. Barely able to see, he turned on the lamp on his dresser. Everything was ready, just as planned. One letter was addressed to his mother, another to his brother and sister. There also was a package for his attorney, the contents being his last will and testament along with keys to a safe deposit box at the Northern Trust Bank containing his stocks and bonds, all left in trust to his niece Dana. She can cash them in and pay for college when she turns eighteen. Why depend on the government for assistance? Besides, in about thirty-five minutes he wouldn't need them anymore anyway.

"Almost time to go," he thought. "I'd better get a move on."

Arthur picked up the morning edition of the Chicago Sun Times, and while leaving his Lincoln Park apartment he scanned the front-page story, "Serial Rapist Strikes Again." A white male, six foot tall and two hundred pounds, had assaulted several women in

1

the area. Beyond a general description the police had no additional leads and the paper said the suspect always wore a ski mask to cover his identity. Arthur didn't have time to get into the story; instead he unfolded the paper, pulled out a handgun from inside his coat and wrapped it in the Sun-Times.

He tucked the paper and gun safely under his arm and strode through the lobby of his building into the brisk cold air that greeted him as he crossed Clark Street. He loved Chicago dearly, the vibrancy and culture of the city made it - in his mind - the most beautiful place in the world, but the recent loss of his wife Rachel had changed everything. No matter what Arthur did, it all seemed hollow without her.

Arthur lost his wife one year ago to the day at approximately 4:35 in the morning. She was about to give birth to their first child, but while on their way to Northwestern Memorial Hospital a drunk driver sped through a red light on Michigan Avenue and struck their vehicle from the passenger side. Rachel and their unborn child were killed instantly, while Arthur suffered severe head trauma and lapsed into a coma that lasted for nearly a month.

He'd not been the same since coming home. Arthur was once a successful advertising executive, very popular and devoted to his wife. Now it seemed as if his old life never existed. Over time it seemed he grew old and bitter. As a constant reminder of his accident he still got horrible migraine headaches, and the prescribed amitriptyline didn't help much. His doctor said that these migraines could last forever or eventually go away on their own, but to Arthur it wasn't the headaches that bothered him; it was the voices. Every time he had one of these nagging headaches he'd hear voices all around him. He decided to see a therapist, fearing he may be going crazy, but nothing changed. Still the voices came, so Arthur kept to himself and rarely left his apartment except to go to Barnes and Noble where he currently worked, or to run minor errands in the neighborhood.

He checked his watch as he neared Lincoln Park.
4:28am
Arthur sat on a bench, closing his eyes.
"It won't be long now my love," he thought. "Soon we will be together once again."

Tears streamed down his face as he reminisced about the life he once knew; the day he proposed to her, their wedding at Holy Family Church on Roosevelt Road, the morning "quickies" they had before heading to work, nights walking together through this very same park, especially the time she told him she was pregnant. He smiled thinking about how wonderful it would be to see her again, longing for her in ways that he couldn't describe.

Arthur opened his eyes.

4:34am.

"It's time," he thought.

Arthur reached into the folded paper and pulled out the handgun, whispered a short prayer and pointed it toward his head when suddenly he felt nauseous, becoming increasingly dizzy and seeing flashes before his eyes. His body wilted from the pain. Arthur knew what was happening.

4:35am.

"Dammit God, you are not going to cheat me out of this!" he screamed at the top of his lungs.

Arthur put the gun to his head again.

"Help me, oh please God, help me!"

Arthur stopped, grabbed his head. A chill run down his neck as he scanned the area. Was that someone calling for help?

"Please help me! He's going to kill me, oh my God!"

Arthur turned, his right hand still clutching his head. It was a woman screaming. He looked around frantically thinking it was someone nearby, but where?

"I'm over here, please help!"

Arthur looked to the other side of the South Pond; there were two figures in some sort of struggle. The larger figure of the two appeared to drag the other into a group of large trees, then disappear from view.

"Please, I don't wanna die!"

Arthur grabbed his gun and ran full speed to the other side and slipped into the group of trees, his head pounding harder than ever. He moved carefully through the darkness, the gun leading the way.

"I can see you, I can see you! Help me!"

In a small clearing Arthur saw a man wearing a ski mask trying to rip off a woman's clothes. He quickly struck the man twice in the head from behind, knocking him unconscious. The man turned out to be the serial rapist mentioned in the morning paper and was promptly arrested once the police arrived. The woman, who was out jogging through the park when she was attacked, seemed unwilling to talk. They both were now in the rear of a squad car heading to the 19th precinct to provide a statement for the police.

"What's your name?" he asked. No answer.

3

She reached into her fanny pack and grabbed a piece of paper and a pen, where she wrote the following note:

"My name is Laura. I am a mute."

Arthur gasped, and almost immediately his migraine went away, never to return.

"Nice to meet you Laura," Arthur said, smiling. "My name is Arthur."

She grabbed his hand and smiled, grateful. And as they held hands in the back seat of the squad car, Arthur decided to check his watch once more.

5:15am.

A new life had begun.

"Nicholas"
By Eve Adamsley
***

I am a believer once again. Imagine that! Me, Bill Turner, a believer at my age! I never thought something like this could ever happen, but this recent incident has breathed new life into me. My focus has changed. I feel rejuvenated, giddy and excited like a child, and it's all because of Nicholas. Sweet Nicholas.

I'm sorry - I know I've babbled on like a lunatic, so let me start from the beginning and explain what I mean.
***

It all started a few nights ago. I was alone at my south side home lying in bed, sipping my favorite drink - Grey Goose Vodka with a shot of OJ - while watching an old Jimmy Stewart movie. It had been an awful month for me thus far, having lost my job and all. I used to be an executive for Bank One until the recent merger with JP Morgan-Chase. It was a position I'd held for years, working my way up from being a teller back when the company was called First National Bank of Chicago. I gave the company everything I had, and for them to announce suddenly that I was being let go after nearly thirty years was hard for me to deal with.

I'm not ready to retire. There's still so much to give, but to what, and to whom? I've spent much of my life working, refusing to do much of anything else. I never married and have lived alone since I moved out of my parents' house years ago. My brother and sister still live in Chicago, but I rarely see them or their kids. I've been invited to come to birthday and holiday gatherings before, but

5

usually I'd just send them gifts and give a phone call. I didn't have time to garner relationships because my job is what kept me happy. I dated a woman briefly about six months ago, but again I let the bank dictate how I spent my nights and weekends. She really liked me too, but she also knew what she wanted. Marilyn deserved someone who would take her out and show her the best that life has to offer, not someone like me – a slave to his job. She was indeed right about me - somewhere along the line you've forgotten what it means to be happy; to smile and laugh out loud. She was right; I'd forgotten how to live, and now what little life I thought I had was gone. Working for the bank was my whole world. Now all I have left to show for it is a large house with few memories.

I must've nodded off at some point while in bed, for I awoke and they were showing that Jimmy Stewart movie again. It was only 11:30, so I decided to get up and make another drink. I was indeed quite inebriated, stumbling around the room with my hands outstretched because I could hardly see. I guess it would've made more sense to put on my glasses, but when you've had a few drinks you tend not to think clearly. Oh well, I'd be right back anyway.

I made my way downstairs and noticed it was snowing heavily, though I still couldn't see very well. I squinted and walked towards the front door and opened it, feeling the cold air rush in. From the looks of things it was going to be quite a bit of snow to shovel in the morning. I can't shovel like I used to due to my sciatica, but fortunately I was smart and bought a snow blower during the fall. I'm sure I'd put it to good use tomorrow.

I shut the door and went to the kitchen, still somewhat unsteady. After making a drink and heading back towards the staircase, the strangest thing happened. As I passed my living room, I saw this big fat guy with a huge beard, legs propped up in the air, sitting in my lounge chair next to the fireplace. On a table next to the chair was a glass of milk sitting on a coaster. My fireplace had been lit; the flames caused the wood to crackle. The room was room nice and warm; the aroma of birch wood filled the air. I rubbed my eyes again and looked at my drink, thinking I needed to stay off the sauce but when my vision cleared the fat guy was still there.

Is this for real?

"Hi there," the fat guy said. "Mind if I join you for a drink?"

He raised his glass of milk.

"Who are you and what are you doing in my house?" I asked, still not believing what I was seeing.

The man smiled.

6

"Oh that's not important. "What is important is why I'm here. I've heard that you've lost your job recently. I thought you could use my help."

"Well, yes I did lose my job recently," I said, sitting down on my couch. "But what does this have to do with you? I don't even know who you are."

The big man sat forward in my chair, extending his right hand.

"I'm sorry for sounding so secretive," he said. "I'm Nicholas, and I'd like to be your friend."

As I reached over and shook his hand, he continued to smile at me. Quite a disarming smile he had. I hadn't seen as warm a smile since my mother was alive. She died back in spring of '69 from pancreatic cancer. My father loved her with all his heart, and after she passed he was never the same. He suffered a stroke ten years later, eventually succumbing to pneumonia in 1980. Despite the loss of two people I loved dearly, wonderful visions of both of them ran through my mind as I sat back, staring at Nicholas. He propped his legs back in the air, a pair of black boots were on his feet as if he'd just come in from outside. A trail of melted snow led from the fireplace to the lounge chair.

"You miss them, don't you?"

"Excuse me?" I said. Was he reading my mind?

"You mother and father. You miss them a lot. I can tell. I've always been able to read you rather well. It's funny, but you've not changed one bit since you were a little boy. I knew your parents too; they were good people. I enjoyed visiting them when I had the chance."

He sat there, stroking his beard with a genuine look of interest. Strange that I didn't remember ever seeing this man, nor did I remember my folks mentioning anyone named Nicholas.

"You knew my mom and dad?" I asked. "That's funny; I thought I knew all of my parents' friends."

"Oh they knew me well. Every year around this time I'd hear from them. I still did, even when they neared death. Normally I'm not supposed to play favorites with people, but I always thought so highly of them. You know why?"

"No."

"Well, no matter how old they got, they always understood the need to maintain a fresh perspective on life. They liked to dance; they went to dinner and took trips together. They were inseparable

7

and loved every day they had together. They lived their lives as best as they could, and I know for a fact they adored their children."

I smiled. "You're right. All those years and I never saw them argue. We were blessed. I remember family trips we took to Florida in my father's 1965 Chevy Impala. I was sixteen when he bought that car, and he never bought another one – not even after my mother passed away. You know I kept that car until after dad died?"

"Yes, yes I remember," Nicholas said. "I also remember you felt guilty for letting it go. You worried about forgetting your parents, but they're still with you, William. They're in your heart, your mind, and your spirit. Those days of loving life, the life you had as a child; you've forgotten what it's like to enjoy it. Quite frankly, you haven't enjoyed being alive since they passed away. That's why I'm here now, to remind you that you are still that beautiful little boy who once loved being William Turner. Regardless of age that kid is still there, deep inside of you. Trust me, I have a nose for this sort of thing."

Nicholas winked at me, touching the side of his nose with his right index finger.

Tears welled up in my eyes as we continued our conversation for the better part of an hour. I couldn't help it, but I suddenly began to feel good again. I didn't have a job and I was still alone, but I felt as if I'd tapped into something that I hadn't felt in a long, long time. I wanted to thank Nicholas, but he waved me off and took a quick gulp of his milk, putting on his heavy red coat.

"Do you have to leave so soon?" I asked. "I'd like you to stay for a while longer if you don't mind."

"Actually it is getting late, William. It's almost midnight, and I have to make a few stops before I go home. If you don't mind, though – I am a bit hungry. Do you have anything I could snack on while I make my last few rounds?"

"Sure, there are some pretzels and potato chips in my pantry that you can have. I think I might have some butternut cookies as well."

"The cookies would be fine," he said.

I found a box of Salerno cookies in the kitchen cupboard and brought them to Nicholas who, strangely enough, was still in the living room, standing by the fireplace.

"Thank you, William. By the way, I have something for you."

Nicholas reached into his pocket and pulled out an envelope, handing it to me. He told me not to open it up until 6am tomorrow, but I would be pleased by what it said. I looked at the envelope when suddenly the living room became dark again. My vision was blurred and I yawned as I began rubbing my eyes.

"Nicholas?" I said, sitting up suddenly in my bed.

It's a Wonderful Life was playing as Jimmy Stewart ran through town shouting to all his neighbors. That's when I remembered it was December 25th – Christmas Day.

I went downstairs to fetch some coffee, a wide smile planted firmly across my face as I passed the living room, when I noticed a white envelope on the floor. I opened it, and it said the following:

Dear William,

Thank you for the milk and cookies. In this letter are three telephone numbers for you to call. Do not try to call the first number today, as they are closed for the holiday, but I know for a fact that Bank of America is looking for someone with your experience to run their accounting department. I'm sure they will find you to be a trustworthy and dependable employee, but try to remember to make time AWAY from the job. All work and no play makes William like he once was! HA!

The second number is to your brother's house. I want you to call him and say you will come by to visit their family for Christmas. Once you've done that you are to call the third number and invite Marilyn to come with you. Like you, she is alone today and is thinking about you right now.
Don't forget what we talked about, for now that you remember what you once lost, you will also remember who I was to you as a child, and that I am the same person today.

Remember the little boy inside of you!

Merry Christmas!
Nicholas

***

So there you have it. I called my brother and had Christmas dinner with my family for the first time in years, with Marilyn at my side. She's really a special person, and I look forward to see her again very soon.

And as I shared with you earlier, at the young age of fifty-five I am a believer once again, and I'd say it proudly to the world.

I believe in Santa Claus.

Paranoia
By Arnold Jackson
***

"If a man harbors any sort of fear, it makes him landlord to a ghost."
- Lloyd Douglas

Recently I'd buried my best friend, Brian Wilkes. During the course of a few months I watched him go from a happy-go-lucky guy to someone I hardly knew anymore. Something set Brian off, making him completely paranoid. For some reason he thought there was a tall, hideous looking monster that was after him; following him around wherever he went. I remember the nights he called my house, begging me to spend the night, not to mention the countless hours of sleep both of us lost because he couldn't accept the fact that no one was out to get him. I took him to five shrinks in less than two months, but he refused to see any of them more than once, rambling on that the "monster" told him if he went back it would kill him. The sad part was Brian truly believed this monster – all the way to the end, when he died of a massive heart attack a few days ago.

I was the 'lucky' one that found him. For the first time in almost a month I didn't get a call from Brian in the middle of the night, so naturally I became rather worried and decided to check on him the next morning. I found Brian slouched over the right side of the chair in front of his computer desk. His eyes held the fear that overcame him, robbed him of his life, or what was left of it. All he wore was his favorite black Nike shorts; vomit was across his chest and on the floor to the right of his corpse. His body was as cold as ice. It was almost as if he'd recently been taken out of a freezer and left out to thaw.

I can recall how I felt when I first saw him – the sense of failure that came over me for not being there with him in his final moments. What a horrible way to die; alone, half naked, covered in his own vomit. His right hand was still holding the mouse to his computer; papers were knocked all over the floor, as was his desktop digital camera. His apartment had been torn apart, as if someone were searching for something.

On Brian's flat screen monitor he left behind a rather strange message typed on Microsoft Word. It said the following: "A_MONSTER shows it all."

I still get chills down my spine when I think about all that happened. This truly was an example of how badly fear can affect the human psyche. As I mentioned before, Brian was normally a happy guy. He cared about people, he loved his job with the insurance company – a job where a year and a half ago he had received a promotion. He was dating someone that he actually considered marrying, and recently moved into a great co-op with a breathtaking view of Central Park.

Everything was going so well, until right before Thanksgiving. That's when his company downsized due to budget cuts, landing him without a job. He began to think the worst and became so fearful of everything, as if his whole world had crashed at once. The sad part was his fear became a self-fulfilling prophecy. It drove everyone away, including his girlfriend Charlene, for he began stalking her. Everywhere she went he followed her, thinking she was about to dump him since he was no longer the "all-important" VP of Marketing at ABC Insurance Company. I recall all the telephone calls where she cried to me on the phone, begging me to do something with him. I tried talking to him, arranging meetings with the two of them and even brought Brian's mother all the way from Poughkeepsie to intervene, but to no avail. Charlene broke it off with him a week before Christmas, which only made matters worse. Brian stopped taking care of himself, sometimes going days without bathing. He also stopped eating, and refused to go anywhere or see anyone except me.

The first psychiatrist I took him to listened intently to his problems, and by the end of the session the doctor diagnosed him as suffering from a severe case of panphobia (the fear of anything and everything) and recommended he be treated immediately,

11

which Brian promptly refused to do. As he left the office in a huff the doctor stood and urged me to recommend he keep a journal of what his days were like, so I could monitor his progress. Perhaps what Brian read at a later time would be enough to convince him that he needed medical attention.   I agreed with the idea and promised the doctor I'd figure a way to get him to do it.

After much coaxing I finally managed to get Brian to keep a journal, and at one point it seemed to be helping. He mentioned to me that he was intending on looking for another job after almost three months of being out of work. For a brief moment it began to look as if things were turning for the better.

It wasn't until after Martin Luther King Jr's birthday when he first told me about the monster.

Brian called me at about one in the morning and said that a monster crawled from under his bed and actually chased him around his bedroom.   I thought he was kidding until he told me he was standing at a pay phone wearing only his pajama bottoms and leather coat, too afraid to go back into his co-op. I had to come all the way from the East Side to get him, and spent the entire night trying to convince him there was no monster, but instead just a horrible dream.

My constant talk that night worked only momentarily. Three nights later the monster came back, and Brian called me continually until a few nights ago. He said the monster wanted him to be miserable and would kill him if he ever tried to make himself better. Naturally I thought that was absurd, and it convinced me to get him some help whether he liked it or not.   I wanted to take him to more doctors, but he refused to seek any therapy. I even tried to have him committed, but when someone came to his co-op for an evaluation he acted as if nothing was wrong. In fact, he even looked the part – his place was immaculate and he was neatly dressed.

"I can certainly appreciate Richard's concern for me, after all – we've been best friends since we were kids. But trust me when I tell you I'm fine! In fact, I have a couple of promising interviews this week," Brian would say, sounding well-rehearsed as Harvey Fierstein in a Broadway play.

As Brian put on his Tony award winning performance, every now and then I would catch him sneaking a glance toward his open closet, as if someone were watching him; making sure he pulled this off correctly. He managed to fool the mental health counselors, but still the nightly telephone calls came. Then they abruptly stopped.

Now Brian was gone at the young age of thirty-four. My best friend, whose life was completely taken over by panphobia, apparently succumbed to fear of his own doing. I cried for three days after his funeral because I was unable to save him. The mental picture of finding his corpse still haunts me to this day. I believe it always will.

Brian's mother, Martha, wanted me to meet her at his co-op and help pack his belongings. Some things she wanted to give away to Goodwill, others she would keep at her home. She offered me several pictures of us together; our days at City College, our high school prom where he and I rented a limo for our dates. Martha even had a shot of us after winning the 800m relay back when we ran track together. After years of friendship and brotherhood all that I had left of him were these photos. I missed him dearly.

In addition to the photos, Martha also offered Brian's diary, and as she stared at the thick black book I could see her hands tremble. I reached out to her, my hands covering hers reassuringly. She raised her head, her bottom lip quivering, looking at me through tear-filled eyes. I could tell she needed a moment of sheer grief, some non-stop crying over her loss. She fell into my arms and finally let herself go. I sat her down on Brian's leather couch and joined her in mourning. I had always been very close to her, even as a kid, and for all practical purposes she was more of a surrogate mother to me. My birth mother passed away within a year after I was born, and my father raised me as best he could, though his job at the Port Authority kept him away at the most obscene hours. I spent a lot of my youth in Brian's house, so much to the point that Martha felt as if she had two sons instead of one. That was precisely why I needed to be there and have that moment with her. Her husband, Lloyd had died almost fifteen years ago, and now Brian was gone. I was all that she had left, and there we sat, holding on to one another for what seemed like hours.

As a matter of fact, I think it was.

***

Later that evening, I took a bottle of wine and stretched out on my terrace. The sublime setting of the East River and the Brooklyn Skyline became my nighttime theater with John Coltrane's "My Favorite Things" gently in the background, taking my mind away from the stress of the day, bringing me to a much better place. With each sip of "Rincon Privado" I felt the uneasiness slip down my body, through my fingertips and into the cool night air, replaced by a feeling of serenity that I thought was long since gone. Make no mistake – I missed Brian, but if there were a good side to his passing, it would be no more suffering for either one of us. For all practical purposes I had become every bit as paranoid as he had been with my constant worrying. "Second-hand tension" is what Martha called it. God knows being a New Yorker can be hard enough for anyone to deal with. If you want to survive in this city you have to know when to cut your losses and keep the nonsense at a minimum. That's a part of living in the "city that never sleeps."

Since I'd been home relaxing I decided to not go out. Yes it was Saturday, but I needed some time to myself. With all that had happened quiet time was hard to come by. Later I would order take-out and maybe watch some television, see what was on American Movie Classics then fall asleep for ten hours or so. Though that sounded like a good plan, every now and then I would glance at Brian's diary sitting over on the dining room table. I had meant to read it hours ago, but there was something about opening that book that made me exceptionally nervous. As erratic as his behavior had become I feared for what was on those pages. All this "monster" business! I could only imagine the twisted things he never shared with me scrawled within the black binding. The horror of his final moments alive! How could he do this, leave behind remnants of his psychosis for Martha and me to deal with? Dying was the easy part. Here we were, left to ponder where we went wrong, how we were presented with the test of being concerned and caring people, only to fail miserably when the time had arrived to prove it.

My moment of serenity left in a hurry. I stood and threw my wine glass over the terrace, then grabbed the diary and thought of tossing it as well when my doorbell rang. For a moment I had been wrapped up in anger over my helplessness, but was jolted back to my senses by the sound.

I hurried to the front door and checked through the peephole. No one was there.

"That's funny," I said aloud. It hadn't taken me that long to get to the door.

I turned and started to walk away when the bell rang again. I pressed my right eye into the peephole again, scanning the full extent of the hallway trying to locate some kid playing a prank when suddenly a huge shadow walked past. I backed away from the door, my body quivering as if I were standing outside hardly dressed in the middle of winter. The room felt very cold all of a sudden. That "second-hand tension" was beginning to rise within me once again.

14

I don't know what made me react as I did, but I took a deep breath and opened the door looking down both sides of the dimly lit hallway. There was no one in sight. As I was about to close the door I looked down and saw an envelope on the floor. "Richard Beck" was written on the outside, and someone had carelessly stuffed the envelope. I shut the front door and went to my living room, glancing again at Brian's diary, then reached inside the envelope and removed three gnarled pieces of paper. After flattening each sheet I noticed the top page was dated "Wednesday April 6," and each page had the same thing written hundreds of times on the front and back, in Brian's handwriting.

"A_MONSTER shows it all."

I reached for the diary and flipped through the pages until I came to the last entry, dated "Tuesday April 5." These papers had been ripped from Brian's diary, but returned to me. Why? Had Brian left this as a message? What was it he wanted to show me? What is it that "A Monster" shows? I didn't understand the message until I remembered it was the same thing that was on Brian's computer when I found him. This couldn't be a coincidence – Brian definitely wanted to warn whoever read his diary.

From that moment on I started to read. Even if you had never seen his descent into mental illness first hand you could tell he was getting worse by his writing. It became less coherent as the days wore on. His entry dated "Tuesday January 18" was his first entry about the monster.

"It crawled out from under my bed with it's thick, talon-like fingers and dark green reptilian skin; its long, pointed tail wagging slowly behind its back. I didn't want to believe it, but this huge creature stood there and stared at me, then growled and quickly came towards me. If I hadn't moved when I did, it would surely have hurt me. After cornering me in my room it stood over me and smiled, showing its fangs that dripped hot saliva that sizzled when it landed on my wood floor. It seemed to like my fear….this thing could taste it. The beast would stop in its tracks and look as if it were pleased, then crawl back under my bed leaving me shivering with fright. If only Richard were here…."

I stopped reading for a moment. I couldn't believe how detailed Brian's description of this Monster was. It was almost as if this being were actually real. Tears began to well up in my eyes again. I had no idea he had grown this bad. I knew he was going through a rough time, but it never dawned on me he had the ability to imagine such a thing. How he became so psychotic so quickly

15

was nearly unfathomable. My hands trembled as I continued to thumb through the diary. The next date I stopped and read was "Thursday March 24th." From what I read Brian appeared to be completely out of his mind:

"The monster is getting meaner and meaner. I don't know why it keeps making me lie to my mom and Richard. It doesn't want me to do anything but wallow in misery. I wanna get out of here, but he won't let me leave. If I had the chance I'd kill him, wrap that tail around his neck and hang him from the ceiling. I HATE HIM! HATE HIM HATE HIM HATE HIM!"

Reading this gave me an eerie feeling. I could almost hear his ranting and raving while he wrote this passage. I couldn't read any further, so I walked back out to the terrace, grabbing my wine bottle and drank it down until I finished it. Those passages kept running through my head, like the sound of echoes while standing on the side of a canyon.

What the hell does it mean?

I decided to give Martha a call and let her know what I'd found. After all – it was she who gave me the diary in the first place. I couldn't help but wonder why she would give me a book with the final entry ripped out, then mysteriously drop it off in front of my apartment and run away from the door. Hopefully she could provide some clarity on the situation.

Martha mentioned before I left Brian's apartment that she would be staying at his place until everything had been moved out. I didn't think that was a good idea given the circumstances, but she insisted on being around as much of Brian as she possibly could, so naturally I found it hard to tell her no. I began dialing.

The first ring buzzed in my ear……

"I shouldn't have left her alone," I thought. Guilt can really be a killer when it wants to be.

The second ring buzzed in my ear….

"She's probably sleeping, though it's only 9:30. I shouldn't have called her so late."

Just as I was about to hang up someone answered the telephone, but instead of hearing a 'hello' there was silence, except for someone wheezing on the other line as if they had horrible asthma. I checked the number I dialed and it was Brian's, so it had to be Martha on the other end of the line. For nearly ten long seconds no one said a word.

"Hello – Martha, are you there?"

That's when I heard the scariest voice of my entire life.

16

"Hello Richard, did you get my note?" the Wheezing Voice said. As before I suddenly felt very cold and started to shiver.

"Who is this? Where is Martha?"

"She's sleeping right now, but if you don't figure out what that message means within the next forty- five minutes and come over here I will give her a fate worse than your friend Brian. I promise you, she will pay DEARLY for your non-compliance!"

My protective nature fully intact, I began to fear for Martha's life. This voice did not sound friendly at all, and I was convinced she would suffer if I didn't come through. I had to, for I'd already let one person die. I couldn't fail a second time.

"Please don't hurt her; she's already been through enough. I'll be over there shortly."

"You'd better. It's just after 9:30, so I suggest you hurry! Remember, Martha's life is in your hands!" CLICK!

I immediately jumped up, threw on my shoes and scrambled out the apartment door, deciding the fastest way to get to the west side was to ride my bike through Central Park. I'd done it before. In fact, my personal best from here to Brian's was twenty-five minutes. Hopefully that would give me enough time to come up with the answer to this mystery. No excuses! This was the time for me to be at my best!

As I rode my bike at lightning speed through the park, my mind careened through an endless stream of possibilities.

"How does 'A Monster' show it all? What am I missing here?"

As I was about to cross Central Park West I saw a woman sitting in a Starbuck's restaurant typing on a silver Dell Laptop computer. She was sitting next to a man, who appeared to be her boyfriend. They were talking and drinking coffee. He reached over and stroked her left cheek with his right hand, causing her to pause from typing, kissing him tenderly. They appeared to be in love, briefly causing me to smile when suddenly I hit the brakes. I'd finally figured out what the wheezing voice on the phone didn't seem to understand.

"A_MONSTER" was a video file attached to an email!

I dropped my bike and ran into the Starbuck's over to the young couple. The sight of a man running full speed at them was rather startling, but I begged to use her computer so I could check my e-mail. I practically had to offer to buy a Mocha Grande to convince her it was important, but fortunately she allowed me to anyway.

17

I took her computer and placed it on my lap so only I could see the screen and sat hunkered down on a brown leather couch. They looked at me as if I were a madman. Perhaps I was.

I signed onto my Verizon account and sure enough there was an email from Brian with an attachment labeled "A_MONSTER." To think, all these days and I'd completely forgotten to check my email.

I opened the file, watching Windows Media Player open. The file was only forty seconds long. Suddenly a picture came up and it was Brian sitting at his computer, dressed exactly as he was when I found him. At first he appeared to be looking for someone, finally focusing on the screen in front of him. Somewhere behind him were blood-curdling screams and a series of crashes. It also sounded as if someone was trying to break down a door. Brian was speaking so fast I could hardly understand him.

"Richard, if you see this email that means I'm probably dead. I've pissed off the monster and I don't think I can keep him from hurting me this time. I told him I wanted to leave and he wouldn't let me, but I think this might be the end for me. I can't control him anymore! I don't want him to hurt anyone else, so listen to what I'm about to say to you."

I shuddered as I watched the screen. I looked quickly at the young couple who seemed interested in what I was looking at. I pulled the computer closer to me, listening intently to Brian's voice.

"The monster is not imagined. It's real, but it can only hurt people if they are truly afraid of it. The Monster is made up of my worst fears and nightmares. Every failure, every wrong thing I've done, every time I allowed paranoia to rule my life – it is a reflection of all these things, and has grown to the point where it's dangerous to anyone who comes into contact with him. You must not allow it to make you afraid. If you ever see him STAND UP TO IT! It's the only way you will survive."

Brian lowered his head, as if in complete shame. The noise was getting louder. Finally he raised his head again – his cheeks were soaked with tears.

"Stand up to it in ways that I was too afraid to."

I started to cry.

"I love you Richard. Please watch over our mother for me."

That's when I heard a loud crash and a horrifying growl. He turned to his right, looked up and screamed, and then hurriedly began typing. Brian grabbed his chest just as the screen went black.

I checked my watch. Fifteen minutes to go two more blocks.

18

Time to put an end to this monster!

***

I took the elevator up to the 21st floor and arrived outside the apartment with three minutes to spare; the door was already cracked open. Inside the room was dark; the air was so cold I could actually see my own breath. I quickly understood what a rack of spare ribs felt like inside a butcher's freezer.

Before I could shut the door a hard slap across the left side of my face sent me flying into Brian's living room wall, crashing to the ground with a huge thud. I collected myself in time to see the hallway light becoming smaller as the door closed, the creaking sound making me forget my throbbing face and remember what I was up against. The Thing that hit me turned the lock and leaned against the heavy door. Though I could hardly make out a shape, I could clearly hear it wheezing; unexpectedly, the breathing turned into a chuckle.

"Did that hurt? I must apologize for being so rude, but I didn't know who you were at first. You could've been a nasty burglar coming to rob me of house and home, and that just won't do!"

"Where's Martha?" I asked.

"Patience, my friend. We've just met, so please allow me to introduce myself. I am the *MONSTER!*"

The Monster emitted a frightening growl, one that caused me to cover my ears in fear. I was never so shaken before in my life, when suddenly Brian's words rang inside my head: *"STAND UP TO IT! It's the only way you will survive."*

The monster's growl returned to a wheeze as it moved carefully through the shadows of the room, it's features barely detectable. It circled the area, stopping in front of the terrace. The doors were open and the curtains flowed behind it as if it had angel wings, but I knew better. It stood behind something that moved. Martha! I could hear her muffled voice; she was obviously gagged and bound. The long and sharp fingers of the creature's right hand grabbed her neck and pulled it back while he held the other above her, ready to strike. The wheezing suddenly became deeper. I knew it was now or never.

"Do you have my answer?" he hissed. "Now's the time, Ricky boy!"

"Yes, I have your answer. But first you must release her and come to me so I can give it to you directly."

"Are you making demands of me, Richard? I am the Monster and I answer to no one. You will answer to me. Come before me now and tell me what *'A Monster Shows It All'* means, and I promise to release this woman."

I walked deeper into the dark, cold room and stopped before the Monster. He gestured me to kneel down, which I did carefully, aware of the dimensions of Brian's living room and felt along the floor until I reached the plug of his touchier lamp, then the socket along the wall.

"What does the phrase mean?" the Monster asked.

"It means your time is up!

I plugged in the lamp and lit up the entire living room. I was face to face with the Monster, who looked like a giant lizard except for one thing--something I was not quite prepared to see.

Its face looked exactly like Brian's!

The Monster screamed loud enough to shake the apartment, covering its eyes with its green, slimy claws. Its tail swung around and knocked me down. I noticed three of Brian's mirrors were lying on the floor, face down. That's where I remembered something else Brian said in the video clip: *"Every failure, every wrong thing I've done, every time I allowed paranoia to rule my life – he is a reflection of all these things."*

The Monster is afraid of its own reflection!

I realized the Monster was afraid of its own reflection, so I grabbed a mirror and turned it on it. It became enraged and threw furniture aside as it came after me. It backed away from me, heading toward the front door, but I cut it off and backed it towards the terrace. My ears nearly burst from its horrible scream, but I held my ground and held the mirror so it faced the Monster until I eventually forced the Monster onto the terrace, and pressed my counterattack until it's back pressed against the concrete edge. Finally it stopped wheezing and stood erect.

"Thank you, Richard," it said, in Brian's voice.

The Monster jumped over the railing and fell twenty-one stories. I heard a loud crash; someone's car alarm went off. It was sprawled out across the hood of someone's vehicle; broken glass and blood was everywhere.

I went to Martha, untied her, and went down to the street where a large crowd had formed on Amsterdam and West 66th Street; sirens wailed off in the distance. I looked at Martha and hugged her tightly; she kissed my left cheek. And as we embraced I thought of something that Franklin Delano Roosevelt said during his inaugural address in 1933, the heart of the depression era. Oddly enough, his famous words gave me a lot of comfort at the present moment.

"We have nothing to fear, but fear itself."

Remembrance
By Roberta Sanchez

***

The fierce October winds blew against my window pane, sounding like a boiling tea kettle. I couldn't sleep; another fitful night's rest was all I had to look forward to tonight. Six months of erratic sleep patterns. For every two days of decent rest I'd get five where I'd hardly close my eyes at all. I've tried everything that I could think of, from sleeping pills to "hot toddies" before bed. Not even a toddy with a healthy dose of Jameson's whiskey could solve my nocturnal dilemma. No matter how hard I tried, I couldn't get any decent sleep. From the way things were going I didn't think it would change anytime soon, so for the third day in a row I gave up my fight. My digital alarm clock read 6:10AM SAT OCT 29.

I got out of bed and poured myself a glass of grapefruit juice and looked at the New York Times on the kitchen table. At least it was the weekend, and for the first time in a long while I had nothing to do. Since January I had taken CPR classes on Saturdays that were offered at Bellevue Hospital, and over the summer I had become certified as an instructor. For the past month I've taught the Heartsaver CPR and First Aid courses sponsored by the American Heart Association, one of the few things I've enjoyed this year, but with all the preparation, plus holding down a full time job during the week, I certainly needed a day off.

Now if I could only get a decent night's sleep, everything would be perfect.

***

I guess no matter what happened, I was doomed to suffer with this wretched case of insomnia until I either got over it or it put me in the Looney Bin. To be honest, that didn't sound half bad when I thought about it. I'd probably be shot up with enough Thorazine to put the entire city to sleep; then maybe I'd be able to get some rest. Ahh, good, solid rest! If only I had some. Then I could relax and completely forget about this useless life I'd been living for months. Hopefully I'd cease to dream, and let the weeks and months pass me by. The next thing I knew I'd be ready to retire, then eventually curl up and die someplace all by myself. I'd be away from people and they wouldn't have to hear from me ever again. That's just how irritated I had become with being in my own skin these days; all of this anger had been building up inside me and I didn't know why. If I could only find a place to lock me up and throw away the key, I'd be the happiest nutcase in existence.

Nope, the Looney Bin didn't sound half bad at all!

I opened my laptop and signed onto my AOL account, "ChiSoxFanNYC." My parents were born and raised on the South Side of Chicago, and though they moved to New York City shortly before I was born, they insisted the only baseball team acceptable in their household was the Chicago White Sox. Friends teased me because I refused to be a Yankee fan, but I remained loyal and was recently rewarded by the White Sox' first World Series Championship in 88 years. My parents never saw their team win. They would have been proud.

AOL finally loaded up. I had replaced the traditional sound bites with quotes from Halloween, my favorite horror flick. When I signed on you could hear the voices of Jaime Lee Curtis and Donald Pleasance:

"Was that the boogeyman?"
"As a matter of fact.....it was!"

For nearly an hour I chatted online with "friends" whom I've never personally met. These were people like me, someone who preferred the impersonal and artificial world of cyberspace as opposed to experiencing the heartache of actually dealing with people directly. There are so many phonies that use this ridiculous service; people who make themselves appear far greater than they really are, telling lies that no one will ever discern to be truth. There are men who say they're five foot eleven and one hundred seventy-five pounds, when they're actually so fat they could fill a room by merely standing in it. The women were no better, sending photos of them wearing pounds of makeup, fake eyelashes and hair

23

extensions that go below their waists. This last visual caused me to chuckle, thinking of something I heard a "real-time" friend say years ago:

"Ladies - listen to me okay? If you're bald head on Sunday...don't go out and suddenly get a full head of hair on Friday!"

I laugh at these things when quite honestly I should be crying. Amid all these crazy thoughts, I'd wasted my time pondering AOL, weaves and hypocritical people. These are not pressing matters in the life of the average New Yorker, but ever since I lost my best friend Daniel Lorenzo in a car accident I've not been right at all. My analyst thinks I'm still in mourning, even though it's been nearly a year since his death; December 23, 2004 to be exact. I was the one who thought there was a time limit on these kinds of things, but as I was starting to realize, you never really get over any of this. You just learn to live with it. Yeah, I realized this was a part of my continued suffering, and one reason why I couldn't sleep. As the anniversary of his death approached, I had mysteriously lost ten pounds in the last month and found it difficult to concentrate on much of anything. Daniel's passing affected all aspects of my life, and I've slowly withdrawn into my own little world, feeling myself slowly becoming crazier by the week.

My eyes filled with tears; another crying fit was coming. I'd encountered so many of these mysterious fits that I could almost time how long I'd be in tears. Through my watery eyesight I saw that it was now 7:02 in the morning. That meant I'd probably cry until 7:15, take a break and continue in the afternoon. I usually cried twice a day, no matter where I was, even at work, so before co-workers saw me lose it I would head to the bathroom for some privacy. The last thing I needed was for my supervisor to catch me blubbering all over my cheap laptop. *"Company equipment is the most important thing here at Legion Realty,"* my boss would say. What an asshole!

I finished my cry and dried my eyes with a Kleenex. Since I'd had so many crying spells I reverted back to my old Boy Scout days of "being prepared" and always kept a pack with me at all times. I took a moment, put my emotions in "time out," as my analyst used to tell me, and tried to make sense of these powerful moments that continued to take me over. What was it that caused this latest fit? Was it about Daniel? It had to be. His death is what triggered all of this, but what was it about his death that disturbed me so? It was just a car accident. They happen every day.

I remember getting a phone call from his mother at around 5:15 Christmas Eve morning telling me Daniel was dead. We had been drinking tequila shots at the local "watering hole" in the neighborhood the night before. We both got pretty wasted that evening, and I told him we should catch a cab home instead of taking his car. He insisted on driving because he didn't want to leave his car out on the street with the dreaded alternate side parking rules in effect.

After I tried to take his keys he got into an argument with someone that led to a nasty fight on the street. My last memory was of me punching some guy in the face and watching him collapse like a sack of potatoes. After that everything went blank - until Daniel's mother awakened me at home with her phone call. I sat up in bed, fully clothed. There was a nasty bruise on my forehead, my knuckles on both hands were swollen and there were scratches across my forearms. My right thigh and knee were pretty banged up as well. When I hobbled to the living room, my front door was wide open. Fortunately no one decided to rob me of house and home.

Mrs. Lorenzo told me that Daniel had been taken to Methodist Hospital in Park Slope. He had lost control of his vehicle and went off the side of the road; the car flipped over twice before it came to a full stop. Sadly he passed away not long after his arrival at the hospital.

Since he and I were so close, and had been since we were in junior high school, I remember how his mother would host birthday parties for both of us at her home since my folks didn't have the space to accommodate all of my friends. Daniel's father died when he was ten years old from liver cancer; he was a well-known, respected and independently wealthy businessman. Mrs. Lorenzo still lived in their house in Park Slope, Brooklyn, a brownstone with six bedrooms, four bathrooms, a full bar in the basement, polished wood floors and windows and a kitchen large enough to feed an entire army. For many years she and Daniel lived by themselves in that house, but since Daniel's death she's actually thought about selling it and buying a condo somewhere. Daniel had two older sisters who lived in Upstate New York, but they weren't interested in keeping this magnificent home in the family. Actually I was interested in the house, but I knew I couldn't afford it on my salary. Besides, my parents paid off their place here in Prospect Heights and left it to me in their will. I had no need for such a large place.

"He came home," said Dr. Loomis. I had an email, but this couldn't be right. This had to be some sort of mistake. The

sender's screen name was "OhDannyBoy" - Daniel's old screen name. I checked the profile info; the exact same as Daniel's. How was that possible? His email had been eliminated months ago.

The subject line on the e-mail said: "Do you..."

That's it! That's all it said. I read the message: "...remember?"

"Do you remember?"

That's all that this message had to say? Do I remember? Do I remember what? What the hell was I supposed to remember?

The screen suddenly went black. It couldn't have been the power; it was still plugged into the A/C power cord. I tapped the keys to 'wake up' the computer, but to no avail. Nothing seemed to work.

There was a horrible screeching sound, then a loud crash. On the screen was footage of a Honda Accord flipping off of a snow covered road. It rolled down a shallow hill and came to a complete stop. I could hear the sputtering of the engine, then finally silence. Again the screen went blank.

I'd just witnessed the accident and subsequent death of my best friend Daniel.

The car screeched again, but this time in my own head, pounding away as if I were being beaten. The pain was so great that I passed out; my forehead slammed onto the computer, knocking loose several keys on the keyboard.

***

I had no idea how long I had been out, but the sound of my front doorbell roused me. I must've been out for a short while. Strangely enough I felt rested, though a bit dazed. The bell rang a second time as I rubbed my eyes and yawned on my way to the door.

Just then something felt different, strange. I looked back at the kitchen table. The glass of grapefruit juice I'd been drinking from wasn't there and my laptop was missing.

I scanned the kitchen for the missing items; searching the floor, under the chairs and the kitchen counter tops. I was so desperate I even checked in the refrigerator to see if, as my mother used to say, the "absent-minded monster" had struck again. Not only were the cup of juice and the laptop not there, I also didn't have any grapefruit juice in the refrigerator. How bizarre!

The bell rang a third time. I hurried to the front door, and to my surprise I found Mrs. Lorenzo on my stoop; a taxi was waiting for her with the rear passenger door open. She held a large box that had duct tape across the top and down the side. It appeared quite heavy. Wait, wasn't she supposed to be in the Dominican Republic? At least I thought that's what she had told me a few weeks ago.

"Here Derek - take this and be careful. It's rather heavy," she said, exhaling now that she'd relieved herself of the box. "I can't stay, sweetheart. I've got to get to JFK before I miss my flight." With that, Gloria made a dash for the taxi. Still somewhat groggy from my nap, I needed to clear up something before she left.

"I thought you left for the DR already. What are you doing here?"

She stopped in her tracks; a look of bewilderment vividly covered her face.

"Derek Jackson, you've had too many shots of Cuervo Gold, haven't you? You and I spoke this morning and I told you I'd bring that box of Daniel's things you asked for. Get a cup of coffee or something and wake up. You've been asleep too long and the day's almost over." In Gloria Lorenzo terms, that meant it was presently sometime around noon. She waved through the open window as the taxi sped off towards the airport.

I looked at the taped box, walked back inside the house and into to the kitchen. The box was rather heavy. Gloria was a lot stronger than I gave her credit for, and in more ways than one. She would have to be after losing her only son, one she loved with all her heart and helped grow into such an honorable man. God, I still can't believe he's gone.

I used a steak knife to cut open the box and under a pile of neatly folded newspapers were several cables, two battery packs and a USB connector. Under a second layer of papers was a Canon iP5200 Inkjet Printer, along with three extra cartridges: two black and one color. I carefully put everything on my kitchen counter and continued sorting through the box. Underneath was a third layer of papers, and on the bottom was a laptop carrying case that looked exactly like the one I bought for Daniel as a gift nearly a year and a half ago. Inside the carrying case was a Dell Laptop computer, the same one I was using.

That couldn't be. How could I go from having this laptop to suddenly receiving it back from Daniel's mother? For that matter, how could I think she'd already left the country when she clearly hadn't left New York? I know I'm hard up for a decent night's rest, but this didn't make sense.

The laptop warmed up quickly. I checked the Internet connection, making sure my wireless router was working properly and I logged in to the New York Times website. I've enjoyed going wireless; it has made using my work computer more convenient since I primarily work from home. I did recall asking Mrs. Lorenzo for Daniel's computer, but it didn't make sense why I'd be receiving it now. There were many things about this day that were making no sense to me. Deja Vu all over again, if you will.

Below the Times logo it read: Updated Saturday October 15, 2005 12:15pm. Stunned, I read that line over and over again, slowly becoming convinced I must be losing my mind. I went to several other news sites: The Washington Post, The USA Today, ESPN and even the National Enquirer. It was indeed true; I was reliving a Saturday morning from two weeks ago!

As improbable as that sounded, it was the only explanation that made any sense. But how? What was it about this day that led me back two weeks? I paced from my kitchen into the living room and back, my thoughts careened through a wide assortment of possibilities. Each time I entered and left the kitchen I stared at the opened box and its former contents, which were spread out across the table. What was the connection here?

For the next hour I continued to mull through an assortment of scenarios. There was a connection between my visions this morning to my present circumstance, but what? Finally the light came on. I turned and stared at the laptop, the same one he asked for help selecting. It was his dream to become a published author. Daniel always had a wild imagination and I had read some of his short stories. I must say they were good - very good, in fact. My last count revealed he'd written fifty-seven short stories and five full novels; the results of years of work that he translated into this laptop. Right before his death he talked about starting his own independent literary press; he had a name picked out: NuDeal Publications. He even asked me to be his copy editor because of my grammatical skills, which I gladly accepted. Unfortunately he never got the chance to fulfill his dream.

I touched the laptop, feeling its cool outer surface, reminiscing about the time spent with him and how excited he was to finally have his own computer. So excited in fact, that later I bought him the carrying case he wanted, but couldn't afford at the time. I tried to convince him to let his mother buy it for him; she'd offered to get the laptop but he refused, stating he was a grown man and could pay his own way. He always had a complex about being in a well-to-do family, especially around me. That was one of the greatest things about him; totally unassuming, always humble.

Maybe there was something about this moment in time that made me want to know more? If I could find the answer to what was bothering me on the inside - the days going without sleep, the stress, the depression – maybe I could move on with my life. I believed within the deepest reaches of my mind there was an answer; I had to find out what it was.

Since I was with him when he bought this laptop, I realized I also had a connection to the carrying case. Maybe that was the key. I picked up the leather case and stared at it. Nothing happened. I tried to concentrate, but the harder I tried the more frustrated I became. I unzipped a compartment meant for storing the battery pack for the laptop. There was a receipt inside. "Just like Daniel to keep the receipt. He hardly threw anything away," I said aloud, smiling at my friend's 'pack-rat' habit.

I flattened the receipt on the table. The case was originally priced at $69.99, but I purchased it while it was on sale at Staples for an additional 40% off. My mother taught me the importance of looking for a good deal, and using those instincts I bought it after sniffing around for a bargain. I was so proud of myself; it took very little to make me happy, and given the high cost of living here in New York one had to be frugal in order to live well. At least that's what my parents always told me.

There was a message at the bottom of the receipt: "DO YOU REMEMBER NOW, DEREK?"

My head throbbed, the sound of squealing tires and the smashing of glass came back with a vengeance. I fell to my knees, doubled over in pain. My hands pressed into my head as if to keep my brain from pushing its way out. I felt as if I were having the worst migraine headache of my life. Not one to get headaches, I'd certainly had my fair share of them as of late. This one, however, was the worst of them all. It was too much.

I passed out again.

***

"Excuse me sir - you forgot your receipt."

The cashier snapped me out of my trance. I was standing in line at Staples Office Superstore holding a large plastic bag; the outstretched hand of a young African American woman in her twenties dangled my receipt in her fingertips. Clearly she had grown impatient, dangling the receipt in front of me, her 'customer service smile' slowly turn to a scowl.

29

"Oh - I'm sorry! Thank you very much," I said, taking the receipt from her, feeling her eyes boring into the back of my head as I walked away.

What a beautiful day it was! Almost like the beginning of summer, perhaps late May or early June. I was wearing a white polo shirt, khaki slacks and my brown pair of Aviator Oxfords that I had purchased from Clarks shoe store in Providence, Rhode Island during the Christmas holiday. The watch on my left wrist wasn't the one I'd recently bought. In fact, this was the watch I had to replace because of the fight Daniel and I were involved in outside the bar.

That's when I remembered what had been happening to me as of late, so I went to a bodega and checked the date on the New York Daily News: it was Saturday June 5, 2004. Looking in the Staples bag I saw the leather carrying case for Daniel's laptop. This was the day that I bought the carrying case, and I was on my way to his place to give it to him as a gift.

"Where is all this going?" I muttered under my breath, walking towards the Atlantic Avenue train station. There must be some message within all of this madness. Subconsciously I was trying to work through something I'd forgotten that possibly involved my best friend's death.   But what on earth could that be?

Some teenage boy trying to beat the light bumped into me and knocked the Staples bag out of my hand. I picked it up and realized I was standing in front of L&M Liquors on Fourth Avenue, which was about a half block from Smitty's Lounge, the place where Daniel and I had been drinking.

A feeling came over me as I stood upright, looking into the picture window littered with announcements of the weekly sales. I walked into the store, perusing the aisles thinking that inside I'd find something important. I'd gone down the aisles and stopped in front of the choices of Tequila. My eyes focused on the different brands, eyeing each one closely until they came to my favorite: Cuervo Gold. My body went cold; I trembled as if standing outside in the middle of winter.

I reached for the half gallon bottle, the squealing of tires blared in my ears again, then the crash. My head throbbed and I thought I was going to be sick. I stumbled over to the clerk and asked if he had a bathroom I could use, then stumbled to the back, wobbling over the toilet bowl; the sound of the crash replayed over and over again in my head. The room seemed to spin as if I were on some merry-go-round gone out of control. I couldn't tell which way was up. One moment I felt as if I were on the ceiling looking at the ground; the next I felt pinned to the floor looking straight up. I grabbed the bowl and vomited. My brain was on fire; my entire body ached. The pain couldn't be much worse.

***

I snapped awake, standing in front of the bathroom mirror and slumped over the sink. My face was wet; evidently I'd splashed water on myself trying to regain my composure. My knuckles were badly bruised, trembling. I ran cold water over them and winced from the shooting pain that shot straight up my arms. I looked at myself in the mirror that suddenly appeared in need of cleaning. I was beginning to think I was losing my mind. First the computer, then the leather carrying case and now the bottle of Cuervo Gold; these were all markers of some odd journey through time. I was hoping that sooner or later this would make sense.

I dried my face and hands with a paper towel from the dispenser and for the first time noticed that I was not dressed in my polo shirt and khakis, but wore a black sweater, blue jeans and black boots. I had a black skull cap on my head, and on the floor was my leather coat and matching gloves. I was dressed for winter. Next to the sink was a brown paper bag, and from the protruding neck of the bottle I could see I'd just bought a half-gallon of Cuervo Gold.

A knock came at the door. I unlocked it, throwing away the paper towel, and to my surprise standing in front of me was Daniel. He too was dressed as if it was cold outside, and from his posture and drooping eyes I'd say he had been drinking. He was wearing the same clothes that he had on the night of the accident, and since my hands were all banged up, I knew that this was the night Daniel and I got into that fight at Smitty's Lounge.

"Yo man, are you ready or what?" Daniel asked, still trying to stand up straight.

I looked at him as if I hadn't seen him in years. "Yeah bro, I'm ready. Let's get out of here."

We left L&M Liquors and walked along 4th Avenue towards his car. Though I wasn't exactly sober myself, I felt competent enough to drive, so I grabbed his right arm before he walked towards the driver side of his Accord.

"Are you sure you're alright? You want me to drive us back?" I asked.

"Nah man, I'm cool."

I kept my eye on him while looking for the cops and put the bottle on the floor. At first Daniel fumbled with the keys, but

31

eventually got the car started. Though we had plenty of space between cars, he still bumped both vehicles parked in front and back of him, laughing at his own clumsiness, while I was feeling less drunk and more worried by the second.

He turned onto Flatbush Avenue heading towards Manhattan, the opposite way from where we lived.

"Dude, where are you going? We live the other way."

"Relax guy. Let's take a short ride on the highway and catch a glimpse of downtown before we get to the crib. You can share with me your secrets about that devastating right hook you gave that punk ass bitch at the bar."

Daniel chuckled. I turned and sat motionless, staring out the window as we entered the Brooklyn-Queens Expressway and zoomed along the East River towards Staten Island.

The view of Manhattan was stunning. I recall the last time I took a ride on the BQE around this time of night. It was a year after September 11th when the lights from where the Twin Towers used to stand shined brightly into the night sky. I remember 9/11 day all too well. I was working on Rector Street at the time and witnessed the second plane strike the south tower. The sounds and sights from that day were forever burned into my mind. Daniel had worked in the north tower of the World Trade Center at the time, but fortunately was away on business, stuck in San Francisco for nearly two weeks when the terrorist attacks happened.

Suddenly the Accord swerved sharply from the right into the middle lane and back and snapped my attention to Daniel. He had fallen asleep behind the wheel.

"Dude, get off on the Prospect Expressway and pull over. I'll drive us home."

"What's wrong D? You scared or something? You think I'll get us into an accident? Stop crying like a little punk and be cool. We'll be home in a minute!"

Daniel jerked the car onto the Prospect Expressway, when suddenly it shimmied, then slid hard to the right. He managed to get control of it before it hit the side of the road. My heart was pounding so hard I thought it would burst through my chest.

"Danny, pull over right now before you kill us both!" I screamed.

He looked at me, eyes burning with rage and punched me in the side of the head.

"SHUT THE FUCK UP!" he roared.

That's when I heard the sound once again, and in an instant I knew what I'd kept bottled up all this time; what was causing my sleepless nights and morose disposition. How I managed to block it out of my mind all of this time I had no idea: I was in the car with Daniel when he had his accident.

Just then the car flipped over and the Cuervo bottle shattered, spraying Tequila all over me as I saw the roof of the car cave in just before being thrown through the windshield. Fortunately I landed on a bed of snow along the Expressway and wasn't badly hurt. Covered with glass and woozy from being bounced around the car I saw the Accord about fifty feet ahead of me, upside down with the front tires spinning, eventually coming to a stop. The engine sputtered, then finally seized.

I stumbled over to the driver side and got down on my knees looking for Daniel. His body was suspended upside down because of the seat belt. He also had a bad gash on his forehead and his leather coat was ripped. Glass was everywhere, and I could clearly smell gasoline. I tried to open the door but couldn't, so I laid on my back, squeezed through the window and reached for the seat belt latch. Daniel's eyes were closed and he wasn't moving, but I didn't have time to wonder if he were dead or alive. My first concern was getting him out before anything serious happened to his vehicle.

After seconds of fidgeting with the buckle I managed to free him, protecting his head as I wriggled him out of the vehicle and onto the side of the road. I checked for a pulse. With one pull I ripped open his shirt open and laid my head on his chest. No heartbeat. I began administering CPR, giving him mouth to mouth then switching to chest compressions when something I had forgotten finally was brought to the surface: This wasn't what happened. This time was different. This time I didn't run away.

When I was thrown from the car before, I smelled of Tequila and feared going to jail, so I left my best friend behind to die, made my way home and stumbled into bed and pushed all of the memories of that horrible accident to the recesses of my thoughts until what remained was only vague, shady images of what had happened the night before   All the sleepless nights and depression I had been experiencing since then was a direct result of my feelings of guilt for leaving Daniel to die like a gutless coward.

But now things had changed. Somehow, I was back in time; but this time I didn't run away, and this time I knew CPR. I had been given another chance and was determined to make the best of it.

"C'mon Danny - you can make it!" I screamed, continuing to press against his chest.

To my relief, Daniel began to move, so I carefully turned his head to the left side in case he became sick, which he did. Not a pretty sight, but for the first time in my life, I was happy to see Danny vomit. Tears of joy rolled down my face as I heard an ambulance and fire trucks off in the distance. Help was on the way. I grabbed Daniel's hand; he gently squeezed back to let me know he was still with me.

"You're gonna make it, Dan!" I said.

That evening Daniel was taken to Methodist Hospital and, thankfully, was in stable condition, and I—well, I was in the bed next to his, with his mother sitting between both of us. She took my hand in hers and thanked me for saving her son's life and for being there when he most needed me. I smiled back at her, and looked at Dan, who was resting peacefully. *Ah, rest*, I thought, and closed my eyes, and promptly began the best night's sleep I had had in a very long time.

Thank God for second chances.

Always
By Edward Urban
***

Nighttime joggers, bound and determined to stay in shape, were running around Fairmount Park in Philadelphia, despite the torrid thunderstorm. They tried their best to avoid running into puddles, but savvy motorists would drive along, purposely looking to splash them and drive away. Some joggers are smart and watched where they ran, however others are not as fortunate and paid the price accordingly. Raymond Tobias looked at them inquisitively, wondering if they realized running outdoors in late October might not be the best of ideas. Ray wasn't outside because he wanted to be; he had an eight-pound Shih Zhu that needed walking. In usual fashion he waited patiently for her to complete her business; after all, Miss Gracie is a princess, and a TRUE princess never hurries. He checked his cell phone. It was almost ten.

Ray was waiting for a call from his younger sister Anne, who was on her way to Philadelphia from Cleveland. For three years Anne had been in an abusive marriage, and after months of Ray's pleading she had summoned up the courage to leave her husband. She was set to arrive by Greyhound bus at Filbert and 10th Street the following morning.

"Can't wait to see her," he thought. "She needs a new start."

Gracie finally decided she'd had enough of the weather and pulled Ray in the direction of his apartment when a huge gust of wind forced the umbrella out of his hand. He picked up Gracie and grabbed his umbrella, dropping his cell phone into a small puddle on the sidewalk. The tune to Claude Debussy's 'Arabesque No. 1' began to chime.

"Damn!" Ray growled, drying the phone on his fleece jacket.

He saw Anne's number on the caller ID, but instead shut it off and rushed across the street to his apartment. He checked his phone after drying off Gracie and poured himself a glass of chardonnay. Fortunately the phone was fine. Anne didn't leave a message, so he called to check her status. She didn't answer. Instead her voice mail picked up.

Roy left a quick message: "Hey kiddo, it's me. Sorry I missed your call. If we don't talk before your arrival I'll see you at the station, okay? Can't wait to see you, sweetie. Bye."

He took a seat in his easy chair and turned his Direct TV to the R&B music channel; as usual, Gracie hopped into his lap. The song 'As' by Stevie Wonder played; Ray smiled because it was Anne's all-time favorite song and often a reason to try out the latest dance together. The two of them had been close since they were kids. She idolized her big brother, wanting to emulate him in every way. They also became one another's confidant; Ray remembered the time he first told Anne he was gay and how afraid he was to tell their parents, who are now deceased. Being the selfless person she was, Anne told them herself, taking away his anxiety. Having a gay son wasn't something that mattered to Ray's parents, as long as he was happy. At first Ray was surprised that Anne had done that, but later was grateful to her for sticking up for him. He loved her dearly.

***

'Arabesque No. 1' chimed away again, stirring Ray from his sleep. The timer on his phone read 12:30am.

Ray grabbed the phone, seeing saw Anne's home number in Cleveland on his caller ID. He would have a few choice words for Richard as he answered the phone.

"Ray, it's Richard." He was crying. "Anne's been in a terrible accident. She was on a bus to Philly when the driver lost control and crashed into a guardrail. The bus flipped over and into a ravine. The Pennsylvania State Police said everyone's dead."

Ray was in shock. His closest friend in the world was gone, and he missed his last opportunity to speak to her. Tears welled up in his eyes.

"Ray?"

"Yes?"

"She was leaving me, wasn't she?"

36

"Yes Richard, she was."

"It figures, the way I treated her and all.......I...I.....I didn't deserve her."

Ray couldn't listen to him any further.

"Richard, excuse me but I need to call you back."

He hung up the phone without waiting for an answer and literally cried himself to sleep from exhaustion. Gracie licked his hands and curled up next to him as he trembled in his slept. She never left his side.

***

Something jarred Ray awake. To his surprise, in the middle of his living room wearing a rain soaked trench coat, blue jeans and white sneakers was Anne. Her bags were on the floor at her sides and she was holding an umbrella in her right hand. Her radiant smile seemed to brighten the room.

"Hello big brother. Shouldn't you be in bed?"

"I'm sorry Anne. I feel so bad that I wasn't there when you needed me."

"Are you kidding me?" she said, kneeling down in front of him. "Ray, you've always been there for me. Ever since we were kids you've always protected me, keeping me out of trouble. Hell, if it weren't for you I never would've gotten the nerve to leave Richard. For that alone I will be eternally grateful. Forgive the pun." She smirked.

Ray caught her meaning and chuckled, holding her right hand. Tears rolled down his face, but still he continued to smile. Even in the afterlife Anne could crack him up. He was going to miss that terribly.

A bright light entered the room, blocking everything out until all he could see was her silhouette. She started walking away, then stopped and faced him once more.

"I'm always here Ray, no matter what. If you ever need to talk to me, I'll be there to listen just like you did for me." She turned again and walked away, the light disappeared from the room completely.

***

"ANNE!" Ray awakened and looked around. She was gone. Gracie was sitting on the floor, eyes fixated on him, her 'feather-duster' tail wagging as he stood. It was going to be a long day for him, as he'd have to deal with the police and assist Richard in making funeral arrangements for Anne. He readied himself to call Richard so he could get more details of where she was located.

37

Working with him on this was something he wasn't looking forward to at all.

"Bleep, Bleep." Ray had a voice mail. He entered his security code and listened; a new message from last night.

"Hi Ray, it's Anne. We just left Youngstown, so I expect to be there on time. I can't wait to get there. The seats on this bus are HORRIBLE! Fortunately I've not had to sit next to anyone on this trip. You know me, I've gotta have my space. Speaking of which, have you gotten a king size bed yet? How do you expect to keep a man with that queen size bed of yours anyhow?"

Ray smiled. Anne always made fun of his Queen sized bed. A queen for a queen she used to say.

"Well, listen big brother, thanks for doing this for me. As always you are in my corner where I need you. I love you so much, but you already know that."

There was a pause.

"With that being said, do I still have to do dishes? BYEEEEEEEEEEE!"

Ray laughed out loud. He felt her warm presence.

"I love you too, little sister."

He listened to the call over again, but as it played he went to his entertainment center and searched through his collection, settling on "Songs In The Key Of Life." He needed this moment, and probably would need several more just like it in the near future, where he would listen to Stevie and think of her -- how beautiful she was, and how much he loved her smile and crazy sense of humor. Ray would need Anne's favorite song to remind him of her gentle spirit and giving nature. She was everything he could ever ask in a sister and then some.

Standing quietly in his living room he heard Anne's favorite song begin to play. And he touched his heart, holding her close and keeping her safe in the place where she would remain, always.

"Three On A Match"
By Ursula Thompkins
***

Match Number One: "Goldberg"

BRRRRRRRRRRIIIIIIIIIIIIINNNNNNNNNGGG!

"Fuck!" The clock on my dresser read eight o'clock. Why the hell does this thing keep waking me up so late at night? This wasn't the first time either.

All the windows in my darkened room were wide open while the storm raged outside. My white drapes were soaking wet and blowing wildly around as if a thousand ghosts had come to haunt. I got out of my bed, wearing only my Pittsburgh Pirates T-shirt and boxers and shut the windows, but there was another breeze coming from the hallway, the wind shrieking like a cat with its tail caught under a rocking chair. To make matters worse, this thunder was really getting to me now. I shivered and grabbed my robe, rubbing my shoulders trying to keep warm. The lightning brightened up the hallway of my parents' house; they should have been home from dinner by now. I wondered why they didn't wake me earlier.

Where were they?

I wrapped my robe tightly around my waist; my fingers felt grimy, sticky. I tried the hallway light; no electricity. Instead I stood by a window in the hallway, waiting for the next flash of lightning so I could see. The flash came, thunder cracked, and I could clearly see my hands.

Blood.

39

"Mom! Dad! Are you guys here?"

I rushed downstairs where "storm ghosts" flew through every window throughout our living room. There was no sign of my parents. I began to panic, fully aware they preferred an early dinner on Friday nights. By now my father was usually half-in-the-bag, sometimes threatening to take out the week's frustrations on my mother. Now that I've graduated college and moved back home I've had the chance to see first-hand what he's been doing to her. For the most part my presence has put a stop to it, though I worry one day it might go too far.

The wind blew through the living room like a wailing cat, so I closed the all windows. But when I stuck my hands in my pockets to warm them, I found a note that said: "Andrew Morley, you killed Frank Anderson."

A cold chill rushed through me. The thought that I could kill anybody was preposterous, except somehow I had someone's blood on my hands. Even so, I didn't know anyone named Frank Anderson so how could I have killed him?

I stood in the darkness, helpless. Lost. I can't find my parents, who should have been home by now. Or I kill them too?

"Mr. Morley?"

In the middle of our kitchen was an island that stored my mother's fine china that she only used on holidays like Thanksgiving and Christmas. The island's top surface was made of marble, and even on the warmest of summers it remained cool to the touch. On the far side of the island was a man sitting quietly in the darkness. He reached into a drawer on the island and grabbed a book of matches. After a failed attempt he struck the match a second time and lit a single candle, his face coming into view only partially. What I saw was a clean-shaven man, probably in his mid to late fifties, neatly cropped silver hair and rectangular wire-rimmed glasses. Despite the candle the darkness hid some of his facial features.

"Hello Mr. Morley, I've been trying to reach you for some time," he said, a welcoming smile across his face. "Please, sit down and join me."

"Where are my parents?" I demanded.

He continued to smile and gestured for me to sit. I did.

"My name is Daniel Goldberg. I'm here to help answer some nagging questions that I'm certain you would like to ask. I'm not here to necessarily give you these answers or tell you what to do, but hopefully I can shed some light on a few issues."

He paused, listening to the storm.

40

"From the looks of things outside, we could all use some light right about now, don't you think?"

He smiled warmly, perhaps the warmest smile I've ever seen.

"Yes…..yes I do have some things I'd like to ask you," I replied. "I feel like I've done something I can't remember."

"What is it that you think you've done?" Mr. Goldberg asked, as he took out a pad of paper and began taking notes.

My clutch on the blood-smeared note was tight.

"I….I think I may have killed somebody," I stammered, a light flutter in my voice. "The scary part is I don't know the person I supposedly killed."

Mr. Goldberg looked up from taking notes and he rubbed his chin.

"Who is it you've supposedly killed?"

I gave him the bloodied paper. Mr. Goldberg ran his eyes run up to the palms of my hands. He glanced at the paper and handed it back to me.

"I can honestly tell you, Mr. Morley, that you've not murdered anyone named Frank Anderson," he said, calmly.

"Well, if I've not murdered Frank Anderson, then what's up with all the blood? Where are my parents? Maybe I've killed them! Do you know something? Is there something that you've not told me?"

"As I mentioned Mr. Morley, my only role here is to help you come to some answers on your own. There may be things that you've forgotten, or memories that are so painful that you don't want to remember them. I want you to take the time now to reflect. Think back very carefully to what you did before you walked into this kitchen. Go as far back as possible, and I'm certain you will find you answer."

The more I tried to remember, the more I didn't want to. Something bad happened before I woke up because of that damned alarm clock. Something horrifying…something…

RING RING! The telephone on the kitchen counter rang loudly. I went to answer it; the voice on the other end sounded very familiar.

"Listen to me, you little bitch! Don't believe one word he says! He's lying to you!" Click!

Something about that voice…I don't know what it was, but I caught a rage that rushed through me like a drug. I faced Mr. Goldberg and grabbed a steak knife lying by the sink – I felt an indescribable hate and wanted to take it all out on him. Funny thing

41

was he sat there with a placid expression, which only infuriated me more.

"Who was that on the phone?" Mr. Goldberg asked. He didn't flinch.

I came at him, right hand holding the knife over my head. I grabbed his throat, ready to plunge the knife deep into his skull when I heard a familiar sound.

BRRRRRRRRRRIIIIIIIIIIIIINNNNNNNNNGGG!

***

Match Number Two: "Mr. And Mrs. Morley"

I jumped out of bed and looked at the clock; once again it read eight o'clock. Fuck, was I just dreaming? If so, I don't know how much more of this I can take. Again there was the nasty storm, the cold air blowing everywhere, drapes billowing throughout my room. As in my previous dream, I shut them, and as before, my hands were covered in blood.

I grabbed my robe, tightening the sash and made my way downstairs. Why were all the windows open? The house was frigid and damp, and my parents still had not arrived home. There was another note in my pocket; I took it out and unfolded it: "Andrew Morley, you killed Thomas Harris."

"I don't know a Thomas Harris!"

"Mr. Morley?" a voice said from the kitchen. I immediately went in.

Sitting on the other end of the island in darkness was a man. I wondered if it was him again.

"Mr. Goldberg?" I asked, straining to see in front of me.

A single match lit, this time lighting two candles that sat in the center of the marble island. It indeed was Mr. Goldberg, his patented tranquil persona intact. This time around I could see him a lot better. He wore a starched white shirt with a navy blue sweater vest. I could see the vest had the "Nautica" ship logo stitched over the left breast.

"Hello Mr. Morley, welcome back," he said. "Please, have a seat so we can chat."

I found a chair and sat calmly, not as agitated as I was before. Maybe I sensed he posed no real threat to me. I looked at the note in my hand, but placed it back into my pocket. I wanted to talk with him a little more about something important. Last time I didn't get that chance.

"I'm scared Mr. Goldberg."

42

"Why are you scared Mr. Morley?" he asked.

"I'm scared because I don't know where my parents are and it's very late. They don't usually take this long when they go out to dinner. Hell, my father is usually on his way to a drunken stupor by now."

"Is that something that bothers you, Mr. Morley? The fact that your father likes to drink a lot?"

"Sometimes, yes. When I was younger Dad was harmless, but now – I don't know. I think he really loved my mother once. She used to do special things for him, like having flowers ready each weekend when he came home from work, or cook wonderful Sunday dinners for all of us. Now those moments are few and far between."

"What caused the change?" Mr. Goldberg asked, rubbing his chin.

"Dad worked for the city public works office. He was out on a job in Duquesne Heights when a large piece of pipe fell from the rear of a truck and crushed his knee. He had a lot of surgeries that helped, but to this day he walks with a cane."

The memory of Dad struggling through years of therapy was hard to think about. Mr. Goldberg sat patiently, waited until I was ready to continue.

"He was forced to take social security disability, something he hates to this day. Since then he's never been the same, and he's abused alcohol, and my mother, ever since. There was one day I came home from school and he had his hands around her throat, and it took all I had in me to break them apart. He said he was angry with her for putting too much spice in his chili. Of course he had been drinking."

"Do you hate your father, Mr. Morley?"

"No, I don't hate him at all. I just wish he wouldn't beat my mother. She's done nothing but love him all of these years. Still does to this day, despite everything. I'm afraid he'll seriously hurt her or she'll decide to leave. If she does, it would be just as well."

"Do you ever blame yourself?" he asked.

"For what?

"For how he treats her?"

"Sometimes, I guess."

"Only sometimes?" He knew I was full of shit; he was right.

"Okay, all of the time. I'm worried something bad might happen. In fact, I feel like something bad has already happened.

43

I've got blood on my hands again and my parents are nowhere to be found. And then there's this."

I pulled out the note. Mr. Goldberg, his hand in between the candles.

"May I see it?" he asked. Just as before, he quickly glanced over the blood-smeared note and handed it back to me.

"Mr. Morley, I can honestly tell you that you've not murdered anyone named Thomas Harris," he said, calmly.

His confidence was almost unnerving. I'd never met anyone as relaxed as he. This was starting to upset me. Why had I received these notes and found blood on my hands if I've not harmed anyone?

RING RING! I answered the phone a second time. Same voice as before.

"Listen to me, you little bitch! Don't believe one word he says! He's lying to you!" Click!

Again, I was filled with a sudden rage. Knife in hand, I snatched an unfazed Goldberg by his neck.

"Was it the same voice as before, Mr. Morley?"

Just as I was about to strike, he said something that simultaneously frightened and angered me: "I'm not finished with you YET, Mr. Morley! I don't give up easily!"

Before I knew it, there was that sound again………
BRRRRRRRRRRRIIIIIIIIIIIIINNNNNNNNNGGG!

***

Match Number Three: "Three's A Charm"

"Damn!"

Without bothering with the windows I jumped up from bed and grabbed my robe, hurrying down the stairs and into the kitchen. I was out of breath as I stared into the darkness, searching for the man who'd strangely enough had become my confidant, even though I showed an equal penchant for unbridled rage toward him by the end of each meeting. He didn't seem to mind though, thank goodness.

"Mr. Goldberg, are you here? Please answer!"

"Relax Mr. Morley, I'm here," he said.

He struck another match. This time around he lit three candles at once, one to his right, one in the center and one to his left. I took my usual seat on the other side of the island.

"Three on a match is bad luck, Mr. Goldberg," I said. "I need all the good luck that I can get right now."

44

Mr. Goldberg laughed as he blew out the match.

"I prefer to think of it as being 'three's a charm'. After all - I don't believe in luck. I actually believe that we all have our place in the world, and as we get older we realize more about who we are and how our gifts help us to find that place. Take me for instance; for many years I've listened to people who have something they wish to share. I have the ability to empathize and make others relaxed when they are in my presence. That is my gift. You happen to be a very gifted young man yourself, and I know once you get past what is holding you back you will find your place as well."

"You really think so?" I asked.

"Yes indeed. By the way, I've heard that expression before, 'three on a match'. I've never been quite clear on what it means."

"It was something my grandfather used to tell me. He fought in World War II and told stories about him being in combat. One superstition that he and other soldiers had was they would never light three cigarettes to one match. Supposedly that made it easy for the enemy to locate their position and attack. I've heard that from other people as well, not just from him."

Mr. Goldberg laughed. "And here I thought 'three-on-a-match' was simply the name of an old Bette Davis movie from the 1930s. I had no idea! See, you've taught me something new as well."

My smile quickly faded as I put my hands in my pockets. Another note, which I had smeared with blood once more. Mr. Goldberg immediately extended his hand, and I handed it to him. He took a much longer look at the note this time, scribbling something on his pad. When he finished he gave it back and said: "Andrew Morley, you killed Edward Robinson." I take it that you don't know an Edward Robinson, am I right?"

Mr. Goldberg sat forward in his chair, awaiting my response. Why? Why was this happening to me?

"Nope, don't know him. Wish I did so I could ask him the whereabouts of Frank Anderson and Thomas Harris."

My joke proved unsuccessful. Even Mr. Goldberg had stopped smiling. He went back to his hurried scribbling as the telephone rang again. I didn't move, knowing it would upset me again. I didn't want to get angry. All I wanted was to find my parents. It continued to ring, but I let it go until Mr. Goldberg stopped writing and stared at me.

"Aren't you going to answer it?"

I shook my head. "Why bother?"

"Because it might be the answer to what's troubling you. But you do what you want. It's your choice."

He went back to scribbling. I let it go for another ten seconds until the constant buzzing nearly made me snatch the cord from the wall. Same voice. I was certain I knew who they were.

"Listen to me, you little bitch! Don't believe one word his says! He's lying to you!" Click!

Again I went for the knife, but this time it wasn't there. I searched the counter when I heard Mr. Goldberg's voice from behind.

"Would this be what you're looking for?" he asked.

He calmly held the knife in his right hand. We stared at one another for what seemed to be hours. He placed the knife on the island and gestured for me to sit down. I did, keeping my anger in check and my eye on that knife.

"The last two times we've met here in this dream world of yours you've showed me a note that says you've murdered someone. Each time the name of that person is different than before, each time you've said you don't know who they are. Is that correct?"

"Yes," I said, seething at his questioning.

"Let me show you these names, and I want you to tell me what they all have in common, alright?"

Mr. Goldberg turned his pad and slowly passed it to me; it read:

Frank
Anderson
Thomas
Harris
Edward
Robinson

I slid it back to him, a perplexed look on my face.

"I have no idea what these names have in common, sir!" I snarled. My anger was reaching a dangerous level. Mr. Goldberg took the pad and made several quick strokes on the pad, then passed it back. This time it read:

<u>F</u>rank
<u>A</u>nderson
<u>T</u>homas
<u>H</u>arris
<u>E</u>dward
<u>R</u>obinson

46

"Two things, Mr. Morley: One, I'm not afraid of you because I know you'd never hurt me; and two, you did not kill Frank Anderson, Thomas Harris or Edward Robinson because these three people do not exist. I underlined the first letter of each name because it spells the name of the person you DID kill."

I dropped the note pad and backed away from the island, my back pressed against the refrigerator.

"That's impossible!" I screamed. The thunder and lightning raged outside as if it too knew the answer. Mr. Goldberg stood from the island and approached me.

"Yes Mr. Morley, you killed YOUR FATHER!"

I had finally remembered what happened. I'd taken a nap and set my alarm clock to wake me at eight o'clock on a Friday evening because I had a job working nights. There was an awful thunderstorm and I heard my parents yelling at each other downstairs. When I went to check on them I heard my father scream at her: "Listen to me, you little bitch! Don't believe one word! He's lying to you." My mother told him that I was concerned and wanted to get him some help for his drinking. He started to beat her just as I ran into the kitchen and tried to break it up. He turned on me, grabbing me around my neck. In defense I grabbed a kitchen knife and stabbed him in the chest; his blood covered my hands. I blacked out after watching his face as he died. That's all I remembered, until now.

My vision cleared. For a moment all I could see was white. I struggled, finally awakening from a hypnotic trance to find my hands and feet in restraints. I was in someone's office, seated in a chair opposite a desk, uncertain exactly what was going on when I heard a familiar voice.

"Mr. Morley, can you hear me?" the voice said.

"Mr. Goldberg? Is that really you?" I asked.

"In the flesh," he said, beaming. Proud.

He gestured to someone behind me. My mother. She hugged and kissed me. I tried to say I'm sorry for what happened, but she stopped me: "Everything is going to be alright," she said as she ran her fingers through my hair. Dr. Daniel Goldberg, MD rose from his leather chair and came around to unshackle me from my seat. My mother sat nearby and nodded at him.

"Now that we have you back, Mr. Morley, let's begin to heal together, shall we?"

"Okay," I said.

I smiled for the first time.

47

The Peril of Rancor

By Bartholomew Palmer

***

A hot Monday morning in the middle of August; the dog days of summer are here. The humidity hung over New York City, doubling as a dense, smothering curtain that contained a foul stench like the door of an oven. Merely standing on the street and waiting for public transportation was enough to cause a heat stroke. Honking horns, traffic at a standstill, people rushing to catch their bus or head underground to the subway. Cars cutting one another off. People roll their windows down just to yell at pedestrians who ran in front of their vehicles. Traffic stops and goes, but motorists here don't care. They run red lights anyway.

Steve Taylor sat and stewed inside his car as he headed to work.

"Doesn't anyone in New York know how to drive? What happened to using the damn crosswalk? If they get hit then my insurance pays for their injuries! Why should I give these ignoramuses a free ride? Let them work for it like I do!"

Steve lives in Brooklyn, but works in Long Island and hates the commute with all his might. In fact, he hates just about everything that deals with New York City. He's originally from Cincinnati, but work sent him here as the newly appointed district manager for United Parcel Service. His wife Melinda, on the other hand, works for Metropolitan Life Insurance Company in Manhattan and loves the big city.

48

His mind raged on while driving down Eastern Parkway, heading to the Jackie Robinson.

"'I love New York', she says. She has an easy commute, that's why she loves this shithole! She takes the number two-train to midtown, while I have to drive over an hour. She should drive everyday like I do, then she'd see how this city really is! Why I have a good mind to….."

SCREEEEEEEEEEEEEEEECH! Steve tried to stop the car, but he was too late. A young black teenager had run in front of his vehicle at the corner of Utica and Eastern Parkway. The boy flopped onto the hood; his head struck the windshield, cracking the glass like a spider's web. Steve's Honda Accord finally stopped and the boy flew ten feet into the air onto the grassy median that separated the main road from the service area and hit the ground with a bone-crushing thud. A hidden object flew from under his shirt onto the service road and slid under a car.

Steve froze behind the wheel. He was shaking, nervous. Fear glued him to his seat. What should he do? A crowd ran to the aid of the boy, while others started toward him.

"Christ, I'd better get outta here."

Steve's car quickly sped away while Roland Brooks lay bleeding from his head and coughing up blood on the grass, both legs crushed and his sternum cracked. He was running from a local street gang who tried to take the three dollars and fifteen cents he had in his pocket. He had taken a loaded .38 Special from his mother's closet and tucked it into his belt. It was never Roland's intention to hurt anybody; he only wanted to scare away the gang that had been after him for months. One gang member in particular, Willie Patterson, had it in for Roland. Willie, closest to the accident, found Roland's gun lying underneath an old Toyota Camry, picked it up and fled the scene, leaving Roland behind in a pool of blood.

Roland had been an honor student at Prospect Heights High School, and was on the basketball team as their starting point guard. He wanted to be a doctor some day and buy his mother a house on Long Island, maybe in Massapequa or Amityville. Roland wanted to make his mother proud.

Roland died before he got to New York Methodist Hospital in Park Slope.

***

Steve spent the day at Roscoe's Tavern just off of President Street and Seventh Avenue; the car parked about two blocks away. He drank Crown Royal with ginger ale until he could hardly stand.

Though it'd been nearly eight hours since the accident, Steve couldn't stop shaking. He had hit a kid and probably killed him and in addition had fled the scene. He was scared that the NYPD would have a field day with him; that is if people from the black community didn't get to him first.

The car was a mess. He was forced to hand wash it since there was no place he could go where someone wouldn't get suspicious by all the blood, yet even after he cleaned it thoroughly it still looked like it was in an accident. Steve couldn't change that. How could he tell Melinda? What would she say? His thoughts swirled in a pool of whiskey and ginger ale when he saw two black police officers walk into the bar towards him. Steve's body quivered violently as they surrounded him.

"Mister Taylor?" asked the man on his right. Both officers looked like linebackers for the New York Jets.

"Yes?"

"We need you to come to the precinct for questioning about a hit and run accident that occurred this morning."

Before Steve could take another swig of his drink, it had been taken from him. "Let's go buddy!" the officer said. He looked pissed off. Steve's fingers felt like they were going to break under the man's grip.

The officers put him in the back of their squad car. Steve could feel the prickly tension in the air. He knew these cops wanted to tear him apart. If that weren't enough, he'd be in a room full of them shortly.

"Great! A bunch of niggers with badges waiting for me. I'm dead." Steve knew better than to say that aloud or he might not make it to the station in one piece.

He was held for interrogation in a room without air-conditioning and smelled of sweaty armpits and half-eaten Chinese food. The place was filthy. Cobwebs hung from the ceiling, the paint had cracked along the walls. Steve was somewhat disappointed, for the "beat me up" rooms looked cleaner on Law and Order. Steve grinned at the thought of Lenny Briscoe walking in, giving him one of his patent sardonic wisecracks. Just then a rather rotund looking black man wearing a short sleeve shirt with a red and blue regimental striped tie entered the room. He wore khakis that desperately needed ironing and cheap loafers that looked as if they were this month's special at Payless Shoe Store.

The officer appeared to be restraining himself. He sat down, placing a thin file on the table. His look meant business. The "Gang

Green" officers walked in behind him and closed the door. Thoughts of Lenny Briscoe were gone along with Steve's cheesy grin.

"Mister Taylor, I'm Detective Marcus Baker. We've brought you here because your vehicle was seen at Utica Avenue and Eastern Parkway where one Roland Brooks was struck this morning. A witness described a white male driving a black Honda Accord with New York plates CDR459 leaving the scene. This is your vehicle, is it not?"

The combination of alcohol and nerves made Steve queasy. He ran to the garbage can in the corner of the room and threw up in it. The detective handed him a towel to wipe his mouth.

"Yes it was me," Steve sobbed. "Is that boy alright?"

"He's dead sir. He never made it to the hospital."

Steve lowered his head.

"I also have some other news for you Mister Taylor. Did you happen to see what that boy was carrying at the time of the accident?"

"No."

"Well Roland had a .38 on him at the time he was struck. It belonged to his mother, who insisted he was never a bad kid. She was right, you know. Honor student, wanting to go to college, the whole bit. Anyway we found this gun on a William Patterson who shot and robbed a woman as she came out of the subway this afternoon. She was on her way home from work when Patterson shot her dead and took her purse. We found him one hour after the shooting. He confessed he found the gun at your accident scene this morning."

"So? What does this have to do with me?" Steve asked.

Detective Baker paused and cleared his throat. "The woman he killed was your wife, Melinda."

Steve froze in shock, then flipped the table and rushed at the detective in a fit of rage. Four officers quickly filled the room and restrained Steve as he kicked and screamed hysterically.

"YOU FUCKING NIGGERS KILLED MY WIFE! I HATE ALL OF YOU! I WISH YOU'D ALL DIE!"

One of the officers knocked Steve out with a single blow and watched as he crumpled to the floor like a sack of potatoes. They immediately put Steve in handcuffs and carried him to a cell.

Detective Baker sadly shook his head, picked up his file and silently left the room.

A Fan of Ms. 45
By Ingrid Davis
***

Move-in Date: Friday, April 15th

Boxes dragged into the apartment. Check! Good china and glassware wrapped into three-week-old newspapers. Check! Call the phone and power company. Check! Contact friends on the status of U-Haul. Oops! They forgot. Make last minute arrangements and rush to pick up U-Haul. Check! Carried heavy boxes down from a fourth floor Manhattan walkup. Check! Placed boxes in the moving truck. Check! Ah! My worthless friends finally show up, just in time to order the gummy Ray's pizza that had been promised in exchange for their services. Supposedly the pizza's better in Brooklyn. That remains to be seen. To be honest, I could hardly wait until this move was over.

I closed on a two-bedroom co-op a few weeks ago, and thank goodness it was out of the madness of Hell's Kitchen. It'll be nice for me to get away from it all – as if "getting away" from anything is possible in Park Slope, Brooklyn. Oh well, I'll take whatever breather I can get.

"One moral victory at a time," as my mother used to say!

I got whatever I could from my sub-par moving crew, who made their way back to the heart of the Big Apple via the Number Two train, but certainly not before they consumed my entire supply of Coronas, and left peeled limes all over my new kitchen floor. I'm looking forward to my new place, and at the very least I hope to select a fresh crop of friends. Believe it or not, my desire to meet new people actually played a role in me wanting to move on. Like the song says – "it's time for a new change", or something like that.

Fortunately this new building has an elevator. No more schlepping up and down tight staircases for me. My apartment overlooks Prospect Park, and from here I can see children playing in a small playground area, their parents reading the latest John Grisham novel, occasionally picking their noses from between the pages to check on 'little Susie' or 'Johnny'. Though it was the middle of April the weather was unseasonably warm, making it perfect for taking a walk along one of many trails that wound around the park. I heard that during the summer there are lots of free concerts and movies shown not too far from here. This park is one of the largest in New York City, and given my penchant for exercise I planned to take full advantage of it. Maybe I'll even get lucky and find the man of my dreams while taking a brisk jog around the park, but if I do that I'd better be careful. "Rudy Mussolini" made it harder to cruise in the parks; one of many things he made hard to do in the city anymore. "America's Mayor" the papers said about Giuliani after September 11th. If they only knew the truth they would reconsider the title.

As customary when I move into a new place I like to say hello to my neighbors. A tenant of a building saying hello to his neighbors in New York, you ask? Strange indeed. But that's what my mid-western upbringing had taught me, and I saw no need to change my ways – not even for 'The City that Never Sleeps'.

I checked my watch. Six-thirty. What a tough way to spend a Friday - unpacking boxes and putting things away. At least my 'slacker' friends helped me put all my furniture in place before they left. My new paint job was completed prior to my move in date, so I could focus on finding a place for everything. Surprisingly I was making good process, but I needed to take a break. I thought there is no time like the present to meet some of my new neighbors, and decided to take my mother's brownies with me as a peace offering. What New Yorker could resist homemade brownies and good conversation?

I took a few napkins and a plate with fourteen perfectly square-cut brownies with me and walked from door to door on my floor without success until I decided to head upstairs. I came to apartment 4G, which was right above my place. I could smell something wonderful coming from inside. The scent of heavy garlic, paprika and adobo caused my nostrils to flare up in delight as I noticed the name on the door said "Arroyo." If the tenant speaks Spanish I'll surprise them with a greeting in their language. Being a high school Spanish teacher does have its privileges.

I rang the buzzer and heard someone say, "I'll be there in just a minute" in Spanish, which caused me to smile. I just hate when I'm right.

A young, rather stern looking woman came to the door dressed in a white t-shirt, black sweat pants, her long black hair in a pony tail. She was wearing an apron that said, "I've got no time for bullshit! KEEP IT MOVING!" I liked her already.

"Can I help you?" she asked in English.

"Buenas noches, señora. Mi nombre es Edmund Cox, y estoy su nuevo vecino abajo. Pensé que yo diría hola y le ofrecería una de las niñas brownies de mi madre. (Good evening, ma'am. My name is Edmund Cox, and I'm your new neighbor downstairs. I thought I'd say hello and offer you one of my mother's brownies).

"Amperio hora! Gracias mucho, y recepción al edificio. Mi nombre es Carmen Arroyo." (Ah! Thank you very much, and welcome to the building. My name is Carmen Arroyo.)

Carmen smiled. She took one of my brownies and gestured for me to come inside, which I obliged. She walked into the kitchen, where I heard the water from her sink begin to run.

"Make yourself comfortable, I'll be right there," she said in English.

Since I was left alone I decided to snoop around. Her apartment was immaculate. The furniture was not the modern type that characterized much of 'yuppie' Park Slope. Instead she had a more traditional look - large wooden chairs with cloth upholstery on the seats and arm rests. I surmised the furniture she had had been passed down within her family; the wood finishing on her living room set appeared seemed well preserved. Prints of Van Gogh sat prominently on her living room walls; Starry Night – one of my personal favorites -- was above her black leather couch. There were several healthy plants set throughout the room, many by the window for sunlight; others appeared to be sitting under special lamps to help them grow.

As I took a seat on her couch my eye caught her entertainment system. A thirty-seven inch flat screen TV was flanked by a Sony HD Blue-Ray DVD player, an RCA VHS recorder, Verizon Fios with a hard drive, a Pioneer amplifier with a multi-disc CD player and what appeared to be a few hundred movies. She also had five BOSE speakers, four of which had been strategically placed in different corners of the room and one center speaker with a sub-woofer. The VHS tapes were neatly organized on one side of the television, the DVDs on the other.

And I thought I was a neat freak!

The sound of water and dishes continued from the kitchen, so I slid toward an open doorway next to the living room and peered into her den. I saw what appeared to be thousands of dollars of video equipment: cameras, tripods, microphones. There were also boxes of film, reel-to-reel players and several small monitors. It almost appeared to be a small studio for editing. Fascinating layout!

"You speak Spanish very well. I can hardly trace an accent," a voice said behind me, in English.

I turned and found Carmen standing next to me holding two glasses of iced tea. She no longer had her apron on.

"Thank you. I've been teaching Spanish for years at the high school level."

"Aha! Then that's why your pronunciation is so proper. Not like us Puerto Ricans who talk too fast and use too much slang, huh? Well it's great nonetheless. Come in and have a seat."

"Thanks. What are you cooking? It smells absolutely wonderful in here."

"I've got a date coming over later. Just a simple dish - arroz con pollo, but with more of my mother's pizzazz. I've also made Puerto Rican Rum Cake filled with chopped pecans."

The thought of eating such a delectable meal almost made me want to be a straight man for an hour—just an hour, though.

"Well if I were your type honey I'd tell you to dump that guy and have me as your dinner date for tonight." Carmen laughed as she took a sip of tea.

"Oh you're my type alright. I can tell," she said. Somehow I believed her.

"Oh really? And how is that possible?" I inquired.

Carmen leaned forward slowly, placing her glass of tea on a coaster sitting on her living room table. She placed her right hand over her right eye, opening her left eye wide.

"How? I've got 'the magic eye' and can see deep into the souls of scoundrels. I can tell a bullshit artist when I see one. I'm kind of like Santa Claus, you know? I know when you've been bad or good."

Carmen's face showed no trace of a smile. She actually started to sing, still covering her eye: "You better watch out, You better not cry, You better not pout, I'm telling you why! Carmen's gonna come and shoot you!"

A sudden urge to run out of the apartment almost got the best of me.

"HAHAHAHA!" Her loud cackle made me shudder. I quickly gathered she wasn't someone to mess around with. Maybe that's what her "keep it moving" apron was really all about.

"You fell for that one, silly," she said, still snickering. I relaxed; a sheepish grin covered my face. That was fucking freaky. She said she was kidding, but I couldn't tell the difference. Oh well, what do you expect? This is New York, where the neurotic is seen as passé.

"I'm sorry if I seemed shocked. It's been a long day of moving, packing and unpacking for me. I'm ready to get it all over with, to tell you the truth, so perhaps I'd better get back to it."

I stood, taking one final gulp of iced tea, when Carmen quickly came around the table.

"You don't have to leave, Ed. You can stay for dinner if you like."

"Well I thought you had a date tonight? Three's a crowd even in Brooklyn, right?"

"Actually I lied. I wanted to see what kind of guy you were before I asked, you know – the whole scoundrel bit and all. I must admit I've found it interesting that you've not made a pass at me by now, which means you're either taken or gay. Which is it?"

"Well… I'm gay, but you needn't worry. I'm as harmless as they come."

"True. I AM kind of seeing someone, just not today. Taking things slowly, you know? I used to have a live-in, but he and I broke up a while ago. As for tonight, it's all about you and me. So let me make it up to you for lying. Why not stay for dinner and cocktails? It's Friday night and we should hang out."

My better sense told me to leave and not come back, but there are two things in the world that could prevent me from using my better judgment: one was a nice strapping young man, and the other was food. Obviously my choice for tonight was the latter.

After heaping portions of Carmen's chicken and rice and a nice slice of Puerto Rican Rum Cake I patted my belly. She was indeed a very good cook. If I met a man that could cook like that there would be no doubt he'd be mine for good.

We made a few cocktails and sat in the living room while *"Majestad Negra"* by Puerto Rican Jazz artist William Cepeda played gently through Carmen's BOSE system. She had lit a few candles and opened the window. A gentle breeze flowed into the room as we sipped spice rum and engaged in casual conversation. She talked at great detail about how she was born and raised in San Juan, Puerto Rico – her father and mother, Jorge and Maria Arroyo, were hard-working people who came to New York when she was nine years old and worked for the City. Her father had been in sanitation; her mother had worked in the clerk's office for New York County. Despite not being well-educated, both Carmen's parents had been fluent in English and had understood the importance of saving money, though they had struggled to make ends meet. She explained when she graduated from high school and was accepted to NYU film school, how her parents had surprised her and wrote her a check for $20,000 towards her education. She loved her parents, especially her father. Though she kept looking for someone special, no one ever quite matched up to daddy. Her father was killed in Spanish Harlem the day before Christmas in 1993. The police never caught the murderer. Her mother passed away shortly thereafter.

After graduating from NYU she worked for Telemundo 19 as an associate film editor, then decided to venture out on her own by producing, filming and directing documentaries – one of which was up for an award at the upcoming Columbus International Film and Video Festival. She took the time to show me some of her work, which I found fascinating. She had three projects going on simultaneously and spent most of her time working, but was hoping to change that once things slowed down for her. The person she was currently seeing, when time allowed, was nice according to her. She hoped things would continue going well.

I shared with her that I'm originally from Bloomington, Illinois – a born and bred Midwesterner who decided to try his luck in the big city. My parents wanted me to stay in Bloomington, or, if I really wanted to be in a big city, at least move to Chicago or St. Louis, obviously much closer to them, but I wanted to see what New York had to offer. After I graduated from the Illinois State University I moved to Manhattan and found a job at Hunter College High School as a Spanish teacher six years ago. At the beginning of the school year I decided to move to Brooklyn, so I took a job at Brooklyn Technical High School teaching AP Spanish and commuted until I found a place to live. It took me a while, but I was patient and satisfied with my choice.

Carmen smiled. She really was an attractive woman. I wondered why she'd never married.

"You sound like a very nice guy, Edmund Cox. I'm glad you decided to share your brownies with me."

"Me too," I said, sitting up from the couch and stretching.

I checked my watch: eleven-thirty. I'd been here for almost five hours, and with a woman, no less! Definitely time to go.

"Well listen, I need to get back to my apartment. I'd like to put a few more things away before I go to bed."

She escorted me to the front door. I stumbled a bit before finally catching my balance. That rum was a little too good.

"Ed, it's been real nice chatting with you. Feel free to stop by anytime. I work when I want, and have no set hours."

"Not a problem, I will. Oh, by the way – you can keep those brownies. God knows I've eaten enough on my own. Return the plate to me when you're done – there's no rush."

"Thank you sweetie, but you won't have to wait much longer. I could eat the rest of them rather easily."

"Glad you liked them. I'll see you soon. Buenas Noches."

"Buenas Noches."

Carmen's front door made a loud thud as I stood in the hallway, taking a moment to stretch and yawn. She seemed nice enough, but I had a hard time getting past that 'seeing eye' bit. Something about that continued to give me the creeps.

That stretch made me a little woozy and I nearly ran into a man who looked like he was just coming home from work. He was dressed in a navy blue Brooks Brothers' suit, a striped regimental tie and holding a black leather briefcase with the initials 'AEW' etched in gold letters. The look on his face told me he was lost in thought, and his reaction to someone standing at the top of the stairs nearly caused him to fall backwards. Not a good way to end a long day.

"Oh, excuse me sir – I'm sorry!" he said, wiping his brow. "I've had a monster day and am looking forward to relaxing."

"Not a problem at all. I'm just heading back to my apartment as well, for I've got to finish unpacking. I'm new here in the building – my name is Edmund Cox."

"Welcome to the building, Mr. Cox. I'm Arnold Willis. I actually live in the apartment you're standing in front of at the moment."

I turned and looked at the front door – number 4A. Right below the apartment number was a sticker with George W. Bush's face on it. The caption below it said: "I voted and all I got was this LOUSY President."

Call me crazy, but I was really starting to like this building.

"Well nice to meet you Arnold, I'll just get out of your way and head home. Drop by apartment 3G when you're not feeling rushed. I've got plenty of whiskey with your name on it."

Arnold smiled and indicated he would take me up on that sometime, but not then. I waved goodbye to him as I went downstairs.

I went inside my apartment, but forgot to check if my mail had started coming, so I fetched my mailbox key and went downstairs. Damned bills! It didn't seem to matter where I moved to; they always seemed to find their way. Such is the life of a young, gay yuppie.

BUZZ! BUZZ! Someone was at someone's front door on the fourth floor. I looked up and saw Carmen ringing Arnold's bell. She fidgeted and looked around as if she were trying to not be seen when the front door opened. I ducked around the corner before she could see me, then peeked up the stairs like one of my hormone-driven students. I felt silly, but I couldn't resist the fact that this might be interesting, so I looked. Arnold answered the door wearing a full-length black silk robe that was wide open, revealing his completely nude body under it. Carmen smiled and walked towards him, her right hand reaching for his throbbing cock in the middle of the hallway. Imagine that! She's even bolder than I am! I watched as she kissed and fondled him at the same time.

"Mmmmmmm, feels like I've got some work to do," she whispered. "I guess you'd better let me in to work my magic."

Without saying a word, Arnold embraced her, his lips still joined to hers. He slowly pulled her into his apartment, allowing the heavy door to slam so loudly that it echoed throughout the stairwell. I snickered at something Carmen said earlier.

"It's Friday night and we should hang out!"

"Something's hanging out, alright!" I said, as I quietly closed my apartment door behind me.

***

A Walk in the Park: Saturday, May 28th

Ah, what a lovely day! The trees were finally showing their leaves, the flowers were blooming and I finally could put on my spring clothes. All the workouts I did over the winter months really helped. I felt good and looked good! That's what's most important, right? Life's too short, and I'm too single. It was time for me to find someone special, but not just anyone. The days of taking the first thing that comes along were over for me, and I truly believed I deserved better. Even as I looked around the park I saw lots of possibilities, but planned to hold out for "the one" – whatever that means. School was almost over, and I was going to do some traveling, beginning with my Barcelona trip in a few weeks.

I really needed to get away from New York for a while. It had been a tough year with all the crime. The police and mayor have had their hands full trying to deal with it all. A few months ago a man named Charles Walker was found dead in Central Park. He was found hogtied and completely naked lying in a clump of bushes. The Times reported he'd been shot in the head with a .45 and died roughly eight hours before he was found. There were two other similar murders in different parts of the City – all the victims were male, found hogtied and nude, and were killed in parks. One murder took place in Van Cortlandt Park in the Bronx, the other at Flushing Meadows Park in Queens. The daily news broadcasts have had a field day, stating New Yorkers haven't been this frightened to go out walking since the "Son of Sam" days. No arrests had been made, and the police had no leads. All of this hung over me like a dark cloud, so getting away for a while would do me some good.

As I looked around the grassy area of the park I couldn't help but notice the handsome guy sitting next to me. He was reading *"Roses Are Red"* by James Patterson, and occasionally would smile at me, then return his glance back to the pages. He was neatly dressed, wearing a black polo shirt, blue jeans and black moccasins. His head was shaved bald, and he had a neatly trimmed goatee and wore rectangular-shaped sunglasses. I tried my best to get his attention, but with me trying to turn over a new leaf I didn't want to seem overbearing. He might not even be gay. Oh well – what the heck! I'll strike up a conversation.

"I've read that book you're reading. I really enjoy Patterson's work."

He looked over to me and smiled again. How about that. He's handsome AND has good teeth to boot! Is this great or what?

"I love his work. The Alex Cross series is the best." he said, extending his hand. "My name is Paul – Paul Darling."

"Yes you are indeed….um…..whoops. Sorry about that. My name's Edmund Cox. Excuse me while I take my foot out of my mouth."

This caused Paul to smile, putting his pearly whites on full display.

"Not a problem. I won't bite – I promise." Paul said.

Well, for someone who just took the word "stupid" to a new level, Paul sure was nice about it. We spent nearly two hours talking about different subjects: books, the weather and jobs. He worked as a librarian for the Brooklyn Public Library over on Eastern Parkway, a job he had held for ten years. You couldn't help but notice his heavy Brooklyn accent, and I asked him if he grew up in the neighborhood, which he did. We kept talking and I knew I had to ask the $100,000 question at some point. I decided to suck it up, take a chance and ask him.

"Forgive me if I'm being forward Paul, but may I ask you something?"

"Sure, whatever you want."

"Are you gay? Because if you are, I'd like to ask you out to dinner, and maybe get married if the food is good. If you aren't gay we can just do the dinner. How does that sound?"

I tried my best at humor. Evidently it was working because Paul actually laughed at that corny shit. Clearly I hadn't lost my touch at cruising.

"Have you used that line before?

I flashed a quick grin and flatly said: "No comment."

Paul snickered like Muttley from the old Hanna and Barbera cartoons and both of us cracked up. This went on for almost a minute; both of us had turned beet red. He wiped tears from his eyes.

"I must say it's quite different than what I'm used to hearing. Now then, to answer your questions, yes I am gay and yes I will go to dinner with you, but only if we split the tab. We'll see about marriage."

Boy was I ever relieved – and lucky, for that matter. A nice looking man like that and single at the same time? Who knows? This could indeed be Mr. Right. We exchanged information and he stood up to leave, stating he had some things to do prior to our date tonight, as did I. As I watched him leave, my mind began to move in full tilt toward the date.   What should I get for the occasion? Some champagne? No, that's too formal. I'll get some wine instead. Shit!

61

I should've asked him whether he prefers white or red. I took off to see if I could catch up with him and find out.

I started to head towards Grand Army Plaza when I saw Paul flagging me down near the opening of a dark tunnel, so I picked up my pace. He clearly had an agitated look on his face and pointed towards a metal dumpster that was nestled between a series of bushes. I looked closely and saw the back of someone's head sticking out from behind the dumpster.

Paul and I walked a half circle around the body and noticed it was a man. He'd been hogtied, a gag still wrapped tightly in his mouth, just like the other bodies mentioned in the paper. The stench led me to believe he'd been here a while. A dead body? Here?

I got a closer look. It was Arnold Willis, my upstairs neighbor!

Paul called the police. I stumbled away, nauseous. My head was spinning and before I knew it a paramedic was reviving me. Paul was by my side, very concerned. A crowd had gathered around the crime scene, while the police cordoned off the marked off area. I touched my forehead, now caked with mud and dry leaves. I had no idea how long I'd been out.

"See, he's fine," Paul said, speaking to the EMT worker who revived me. "He's just not used to seeing a dead body."

"Oh, and I guess you're used to that sort of thing?" I asked.

"Dead body, lousy lay – minus the smell, they're almost synonymous."

I could see Paul has a similar sense of humor like I do, along with a bad sense of timing – also very much like me. Maybe that's why I was starting to like him.

I managed a weak smile and was offered a cup of water, which I drank down like a shot of tequila. As Paul helped me to my feet I looked around at the people gathered like cattle and noticed Carmen was standing silently in front of the crowd. She appeared to be out for a walk, dressed in a white jogging suit and matching white New Balance sneakers. There were straps of a dark green backpack strewn over her shoulders, and she was carrying a small black box, holding it steadily towards the crime scene. From the expression on her face, this didn't appear to be one of her better days, I would say.

"Carmen, are you alright?" I asked, walking towards her. My head began to pound from the smelling salts.

Carmen looked past me and saw the EMT workers zip up the body bag that contained Arnold's corpse. As they walked by her she started to cry, then ran away.

"Carmen! Wait!" I yelled, to no avail.

She ran up the hill and completely out of sight.   Oh well, I'd get back with her later. Paul touched my shoulder gently, his face riddled with concern.

"I've already spoken to the police, so we can go. Are you going to be alright?" he asked.

"Yes, I'll be fine, though I'm sure others in the building will take this hard. Arnold was a well-liked person. He had no kids and was never married, but had been very active in community events from what I was told."

Paul began to rub my back, then looked off in Carmen's direction.

"She gonna be alright?"

"She'll be fine. We're friends. I'll talk to her about it. She obviously is going to need some time to herself. I'll grant her that."

I turned towards him, and in a surprising move, even by me, I kissed Paul and placed my hands on his broad, muscular shoulders. I was beginning to feel very comfortable with him already.

"But before I talk to her, you and I have a date tonight.   I'll expect you at my place, nicely dressed, smelling good and ready to have a nice evening."

I took his hand and we walked away from the spectacle by ourselves. Could this be Mr. Right? Only time will tell.

***

The Discovery: Friday, July 15th

As I looked to my right I could see the Manhattan skyline, all lit up in its glory on a warm summer night. Despite the tragic events of 9-11, the view was still breathtaking. Manhattan is the most densely populated of all the five boroughs, but it never seems to matter when I look at the Empire State and Chrysler Buildings as they stand proudly against the starry night sky. I've often imagined being there with a special person, my arm around their shoulder looking over New York City, feeling as if we were kings presiding proudly over our kingdom.

These thoughts, and more, flowed freely as I reminisced on my previous two weeks in Spain. Coming home from a long vacation was not the greatest thing; in fact, for me it's usually pretty depressing. However, this time was different because I had a traveling companion. Next to me in back of the taxi, Paul was sleeping very peacefully. Poor thing! He'd never traveled overseas before, and though he enjoyed himself, all the running around we did together wore him out. Oh well – very soon we'd be home and he could get a good night's rest.

The taxi made it from LaGuardia Airport to the apartment in roughly a half hour, which was good given the heavy 9pm traffic into the City. After bringing our suitcases inside I undressed an incoherent Paul and put him to bed, then headed to see what "goodies" were in store for me at the mailbox. What I saw didn't shock me in the least! Bills, bills, bills!

I went through the huge pile, mostly junk mail. I also saw a postcard that came from Spain, but didn't recognize it since I hadn't sent one to my own address. It was from Paul, that little sneak! It said the following:

Dear Eddie:

I'm so happy I decided to come to Prospect Park that Saturday in May. My life has never been more complete since I've been with you.

Love you,
Paulie

I felt an incredible rush come over me. After all the lousy dates and one-niters, I truly believed I'd finally found someone special. The timing of this lovely card was perfect. While we were in Spain I had been thinking about asking him to move in with me – quite a transformation from my previous 'confirmed bachelor' life engrossed in frivolity. When he mentioned to me a few weeks earlier that his lease was about to expire, I decided to give our two weeks together a chance before broaching the topic. Thanks to Paul and his loving gesture my mind was made up. I wanted him with me forever.

I came across a letter that was addressed to Carmen, reminding me I'd forgotten to call her before I left on my trip. At first she seemed down, but later acted as if nothing happened. In fact, for about a solid month I saw a parade of men going in and out of her apartment almost daily. Many nights Paul and I would hear loud music above us; then it would get quiet, only to later hear Carmen's screams of passion and a steady thumping. Sometimes it caused us to crack up a bit; at other times it would get on our nerves. Carmen had a sexual appetite with no limits. We'd awaken at 2:30

64

in the morning hearing her blurt out in Spanish "sí papá, démelo papa" ("yes daddy, give it to me daddy"), while her headboard pounded against the wall.   That's one of the problems with understanding Spanish – you tend to hear and understand more than you really need to.

I took a closer look at the letter. It came from the Columbia University Alumni Association and was addressed to one Charles Walker. I checked the address again to make sure it wasn't to another tenant, but indeed it was Carmen's address. Charles Walker? That name seemed familiar. It took a few minutes before I realized where I'd heard that name before.

I dropped the remaining mail on my dining room table and went to my computer, typing 'Charles Walker' and 'hogtied' into Google. What pulled up were several news articles identifying Charles Walker being killed by the "Hogtie Murderer" in Central Park, New York. Thinking the name had to be a coincidence I typed in 'Charles Walker' and 'Columbia University'. This time Google pulled up an obituary from the Daily News for a Charles Walker, age forty-four, who was a tenured professor at Columbia University. The cause of death was not mentioned, but the month of his passing was January – *the same as the murder!* This couldn't be a mere coincidence. This had to be the same person.

For an hour I paced my living room, thinking about all the times that Carmen and I were together, the things we discussed and what she had shown me. What did I know about her? Her parents were from Puerto Rico and were city workers, but they had both passed away; she went to NYU and studied film and did freelance documentaries; she also mentioned having a live-in boyfriend. *Could this boyfriend have been the murdered Charles Walker? And if the killer was Carmen, could she also have done in Arnold Willis? WAIT! Her father!* She said a mugger in Washington Heights had murdered him – but how? I decided to look online.

I combed the net, searching for any information regarding Jorge Arroyo's death but found nothing. Now that I thought about it, the 'Net might not have anything because it was such an old story. *Paul! He could look up the story for me on microfiche!* I'm sure the library would have it stored some place. If I gave him the information he could take it to work with him on Monday.

I scrambled into the bedroom and turned on the reading light above the bed. I was sorry to wake him, but I couldn't keep what I knew to myself until the next day. He groaned, and rubbed his eyes. Poor thing – I felt terrible for doing this to him.

"Huh? What's going on babe?" he mumbled.

"Sweetie, I'm going to tell you something important and I need you to pay close attention, alright?"

He sat up in bed and folded his arms.

"Alright, since it can't wait until later – what is it?"

Paul patiently listened as I explained everything to him; the murders, her boyfriend's name and occupation, the death of her father. His expression softened; I think he began to understand the connection.

"So you'd like for me to check the newspapers back in December of 1993, right?"

"Yes, please. If there's a way to connect her father's death to Charles Walker and Arnold Willis then we'll go to the police with what we know. In the meantime, don't dare say anything about Charles Walker's mail coming to our mailbox. We don't want to set her off until this information is verified."

Paul nodded, smiled. "You're quite the detective, aren't you? I had no idea I was getting involved with a 'Hercule Poirot' type."

I raised my left eyebrow and, in my best French accent, calmly said: *"yes you are right mon ami, the sky is blue, the sun is shining, and yet you forget that everywhere…there is evil under the sun."*

I gave Paul a kiss, one of many for the next two hours.

***

A Toast to the Past: Saturday, July 23rd

It didn't take long for Paul to find the information we needed. He gave me a call at home to inform me of his discovery. In the December 25, 1993 edition of the New York Post was a short article that read:

On Friday, December 24th Jorge Alejandro Arroyo of Washington Heights was killed as he was exiting a grocery store at the corner of East 117th street and 5th Avenue. Witnesses say Mr. Arroyo was holding a bag of groceries in his hand when an unknown suspect approached him wearing a black jumpsuit, ski mask and sneakers and fired three shots directly into his chest, then fled the scene. The police say nothing was taken from Mr. Arroyo. Witnesses stated the perpetrator was carrying a small, rectangular box during the shooting. Thus far no arrests have been made and the police are making inquiries. Mr. Arroyo is survived by his daughter Carmen and wife Maria of Spanish Harlem. He was forty-seven years old.

As Paul and I combed through every word in this article we both looked at each other thinking the same exact thing. The report made mention of a "small, rectangular object" that sounded just like what Carmen was holding at the crime scene for Arnold Willis' murder. The "Hogtie Murderer" had to be her; there was no doubt about it. Now it was time for action!

I called the 25th precinct and spoke to a desk sergeant, letting him know I might have some valuable information regarding the recent murders and one of their cold cases. After several calls during the course of the week I finally heard from Detective Mark Logan who said he was the original detective for the Arroyo case back in 1993. He mentioned he wanted to come speak to Paul and me about this matter, and if what we had was good enough he'd re-open the case. He and his partner, Detective Dean Craig, arrived around three that afternoon.

Paul and I explained everything from the beginning. As Detective Logan took notes on a notepad, I told him everything we had talked about during my first encounter with her; the fact that she was having a secret affair with one of the murder victims and her odd behavior in Prospect Park. I even mentioned the misdelivered mail. Paul showed them the newspaper article and we both noted seeing Carmen holding a black box that appeared to be pointed directly at the crime scene. Though we had no idea what the box was for, both of us shared with the police that given the fact she produces documentaries for a living she might be filming something.

Maybe she filmed her victims as they were being murdered!

"Where does this woman live again?" Detective Logan asked me.

"She lives directly above me, Detective. I tell you, I'm really starting to believe she's the person who's behind all of this."

"Well, you may be right," Detective Craig said. "The person who murdered Jorge Arroyo years ago shot him with a .45. The gun was never recovered, but we know it because of the autopsy. The bullets definitely came from someone who owned that weapon."

Paul and I looked at each other. There seemed to be enough information to go on. And to think, both of us had been around her, completely unaware that we could be in grave danger.

"I think I've got enough here to re-open this case. Since she's from East Harlem and all the extenuating circumstances we may be on to something. We'll keep in touch with you. Thanks for contacting us."

The detectives stood, shaking our hands as they prepared to leave when suddenly a loud series of screams came from upstairs in Carmen's apartment. These weren't screams from Carmen's overactive libido, but instead someone sounded as if they were being attacked. The detectives instinctively rushed out the door and headed up the stairs two at a time. Paul and I slid out behind them.

As we made it to the top of the staircase Detective Logan pointed to Carmen's apartment, which I nodded. He waved us away, both detectives removing their revolvers and knocking on the door. The screaming, along with a buzzing sound, continued to fill the entire hall.

"Open the door, ma'am! It's the police!" Detective Craig said, in a voice that made both Paul and me tremble. These two guys were no pushovers.

As they stepped back from the door it immediately became very quiet in the apartment. I could see the faces of the detectives – very stern, cold and emotionless. They looked like they were ready for trouble – trouble in the name of Carmen.

The door to the apartment opened and Carmen stuck her head from around the corner, a look of complete surprise on her face. She looked at both men and saw us standing behind them. Paul and I stood perfectly still; the tension in the hallway was so heavy you could cut it with a knife. Finally Carmen came from behind the door, allowing it to nearly close behind her. She was wearing her usual lounge wear – gray sweat pants and a t-shirt that said "Don't ask me for s$%t!"

"Can I help you gentlemen?"

"Ma'am we're sorry to disturb you. I am Detective Mark Logan of the 33rd precinct and this is Detective Dean Craig. We heard loud screaming coming from your apartment. Would you mind if we came in to take a look around?"

"No problem, please come in. You too, Paul and Ed!"

We looked at one another uneasily. The detectives had already entered the apartment and Carmen stood aside allowing us to pass. She visibly looked agitated, and I wondered if she suspected we knew the truth about her, or maybe she was just pissed about being disturbed from whatever she was doing. Either way, I began thinking this was probably the beginning of the end of our friendship.

As always the apartment was immaculate. Not a speck of dust anywhere, nor was anything out of place. Her plants looked healthy and the television was on, but the volume was had been muted. The detectives looked around the living room. Detective Logan reviewed her selection of movies, occasionally grabbing a DVD out of its place and looking at the back of the case. Detective Craig walked into the kitchen and looked around. On the kitchen table was a half-eaten sandwich on a plate sitting next to an empty glass.

"I'm afraid I caused you gentlemen some trouble. I fell asleep and rolled over on the remote control, which turned up the volume of the stereo. I was watching 'A Texas Chainsaw Massacre' and I guess in addition to scaring myself I caused you guys to come running up here."

"That's alright ma'am, we came here to see these two gentlemen for an unrelated matter. Completely understandable," Detective Craig replied, coming from the kitchen.

Logan was still looking though her movie selection. He and Craig made eye contact. What he said next made me shudder.

"I see you have a lot of horror films here in your collection…Halloween, Scream, Carrie, The Shining, Psycho. You seem like a huge fan, just like me."

He slid one particular film from the entertainment center and raised it so everyone could see what it was.

"Ms. 45! Now here's a cult classic if I ever saw one. Hey Dean – you ever see this movie?"

Paul and I watched the detectives interact like we were viewing a tennis match. We didn't say a word, taking a glance at Craig. Carmen looked at him as well - a blank expression on her face.

"Yeah – isn't that the film about that girl who was raped twice in the same day, then kills her second attacker? It's been a while, but I think she beat the guy to death with an iron, right?"

"Yeah, but you know what? She stole the gun the second rapist held her hostage with and went on a shooting spree – looking for men to kill wherever she could find them. A group of thugs tried to attack her in Central Park and she shot all of them."

I stepped back and reached for Paul's hand. This mindless chatter was headed somewhere. These cops were trying to put the squeeze on Carmen, and I basically wanted to leave them to it. Paul however seemed intrigued by all of this. He didn't move an inch and watched everything very intently.

"Yeah that's right. The gun she used in the movies was a .45, hence, of course, the title," Logan replied.

He slid the DVD back in its place. Logan took a step away from the entertainment center, pulling out his notepad. Craig walked back into the living room and stood next to him. Carmen stood perfectly still as did we. These two guys were definitely in control of the situation.

"Miss Arroyo, is that right?"

"Yes."

"Do you know a Charles Walker or an Arnold Willis?"

"Yes, Charles Walker used to live here until we broke up, and Arnold Willis and I dated for a while. Charles died earlier this year from a heart attack."

Carmen gave Paul and me a menacing look before returning her gaze back towards Logan. He noted the look as he continued his questioning.

"You know several murders have taken place involving men who were hogtied and left for dead. They were found in a park, stripped naked and shot in the head with a .45."

"And what? You think because I own a movie called 'Ms. 45' I killed those men? You guys must really be getting desperate."

"Ma'am, we're only asking questions at this point. No one is accusing you of anything, but we would appreciate it if you could do us a favor. Do you still have anything of Charles Walker's that can positively identify him, like maybe a photograph? We just want to make sure we have the right peerson."

"Yes, I have an article he wrote for the Columbia University newspaper about two years ago that has his picture on it. It's in my bedroom – I'll be right back."

Carmen disappeared around the corner, heading towards her bedroom while the four of us stood around waiting for her return. Before she came back I went to her kitchen. My throat was dry and I was rather nervous with being here, so I wanted to get a glass of water. I picked up the empty glass and was just opening the refrigerator when Carmen came rushing into the kitchen and slammed the refrigerator door closed. The sound was so loud the detectives and Paul came in as well. Carmen looked very nervous, but tried her best to recover.

"Ed, you know I like to serve my guests myself!" she snapped.

She had never done that before. After our first meeting she could care less if I went in her refrigerator or not. Something was up, and the detectives knew it. I moved out of the way.

"May I have a glass of water too?" Logan said, taking the newspaper article from her right hand.

No one moved. Logan stared at Carmen with the same look he had in the hallway. Carmen looked like she'd been caught, when suddenly Detective Craig's cell phone rang. He stepped back into the living room while Logan glanced at the newspaper, still waiting on his glass of water. Carmen slowly reached for door and grabbed her water pitcher, trying not to let anyone see what she had inside, clearly sweating. I thought I was about to pass out. Paul still looked as calm as ever.

"Excuse me everyone; Mark can I see you out here please!" Detective Craig said, grabbing Logan's arm.

Carmen again looked at both of us with great disdain. She slammed the refrigerator door, not taking her eyes off of us while she poured the detective a glass of water. After she filled the glass she stood with the glass in hand, waiting for the detectives' return. I was a nervous wreck, and swallowed hard as both men came back into the kitchen.

"I'm sorry Ms. Arroyo, we need to leave right now. Please forgive us for disturbing you," Logan said, handing her back the newspaper.

Detective Craig motioned for us to follow him outside the apartment. I was grateful to leave, but I could still feel Carmen's eyes burning into my back. As I turned to close the door she stood in the hallway perfectly still - staring at me, then very slowly she raised her right hand, covering her right eye while opening her left as wide as she did before the day we first met. Carmen raised her left hand, giving me "the gun", then turned and walked back into the kitchen. I thought I would shit my pants.

Paul was talking to the detectives by the staircase. Detective Craig was informing him on what took place.

"Gentlemen it seems we've arrested the 'Hogtie Murderer.' I just received a phone call from my precinct. Another of our detectives responded to a call from a half-naked man running out of an apartment building in the upper west side. When the officers responded to the scene they searched the suspect's apartment and the woman who lived there confessed to the murders. A .45 revolver was recovered. Oh, and by the way – the murdered Charles Walker was white, not black – as was the Charles Walker in her newspaper article. I guess your hunch was incorrect."

The detectives went back to the City. Paul and I were shocked. We truly thought Carmen was guilty. It looked like we had some serious apologizing to do. I doubted if she would ever forgive us.

"Oh well – so much for Hercule Poirot," I said.

Paul smiled. He took my hand and kissed it.

"That's ok; at least the killer's days are over. Now tonight I think I'll take the 'ex-sleuth' out to dinner, and together we'll figure out how to make it up to Carmen later, alright?"

"Okay," I said, as Paul took me by the hand and walked silently with me back to the apartment.

It was sure nice having him here in my life. I am such a lucky man.

***

As Ed closed her front door Carmen went back into the kitchen, took the glass of water she originally poured for the detective and drank it straight down.

"That was close!" she thought as she opened the refrigerator door and took out her father's .45 revolver, which was sitting on the second shelf in the back.

She poured herself a shot of tequila and grabbed a lime from the refrigerator, leaving the bottle on the kitchen table. She then brought the gun with her into the living room. Carmen sat on the couch, placing the gun on her lap and reached for her remote. It was a good thing she was able to switch from VCR to DVD so quickly or otherwise they would've seen what she was *really* looking at just before the police came banging on her door. She pressed play on the VCR and began watching footage she took using a small camera that she kept secured in a rectangular black box. The tape began to play. Someone was holding a camera at waist level, filming themselves walking through a crowd on the street when they came to a stop outside a corner grocery store. Just then out walks Jorge Alejandro Arroyo – Carmen's father!

"Hello daddy," her voice said on the tape, the gun pointed at him in front of the camera.

"Sweetie, *please*......put the gun down!"

POW! POW! POW!

People screamed as Carmen ran away from the scene, the camera bouncing wildly around. The screen went black.

A sudden burst of adrenaline hit Carmen, causing her to stand and shout at the television screen: "Happy Birthday to my daddy, the man who raped me all those years and thought he would get away with it!"

Carmen went back to the kitchen, sprinkled her left hand with salt, grabbing the tequila and lime. Carmen raised her shot glass.

"A toast to me – the REAL Ms. 45 – in the flesh, baby!"

Carmen licked the salt, gulped down the tequila and bit heartily into the lime, then suddenly began to sing with glee, covering her right eye, her left opened wide: "You better not shout, You better not cry, You better not pout, I'm telling you why! Carmen's gonna come and – SHOOT YOU!"

Ten Twenty-Four
By Quincy Powell
***

On a warm and sultry Friday evening in New York City a very tired Alex Bixby made his way home after a long day at work. He strode along Prospect Park West in Brooklyn towards his apartment as sweat trickled down his forehead; his white L.L. Bean button-down shirt and khaki pants clung to his body. The only thing that kept him going were thoughts of sitting in his easy chair with a glass of Jameson whiskey on the rocks, and with this visual in mind, his steps became quicker as he approached the building.

"I'm finally home," he thought, wide smile across his face.

Alex stopped briefly to check his mailbox, then entered his air-conditioned apartment, relieved to be out of that oven, also known as the outdoors. He took a quick shower and put on his favorite navy blue shorts and t-shirt that said "Illinois," for the University of Illinois at Urbana-Champaign, his alma mater. The next task was to decide between leftover chicken and rice or Nathan's hotdogs and B&M baked beans for dinner.

"It's Friday. I think I'll keep it simple," he thought, deciding on the hotdogs and beans.

Alex grabbed the bottle of whiskey from his pantry closet and made a drink while he waited for the beans to cook on the stove. The New York Yankees were playing the Boston Red Sox, and he took several huge gulps as he listened to Michael Kay's commentary.

Despite his Midwestern roots, the Red Sox were his favorite baseball team.

"That ball is deep into right field, way back…. SEE YA! A home run for David Ortiz!"

Alex smiled and poured himself another drink and took a sip. He enjoyed the warm sensation that coursed through his veins from the alcohol. He closed his eyes and took a series of deep breaths as he could feel his body slowly relax, letting go of the stress from the past week. Moments later his serenity was interrupted from his front door buzzer.

"Come in!" he shouted, opening his eyes.

An older man, roughly 5 foot 8 inches tall, bearded and wearing a fireman's coat and hat came through the door. Alex didn't know this person and tried to stand when the man, who had an engaging smile on his face, gestured him to sit.

"Please, please, sit down. I don't mean to interrupt your game," the man said calmly. "I simply wanted to drop by and introduce myself. I've moved next door."

"Oh hello," Alex said, shaking his hand. "My name is Alex Bixby."

"Nice to meet you, Alex. I'm Fred, and as you can probably tell, I'm a fireman. Sorry for coming over in my work clothes, but there are painters working late in my apartment and I'm trying to stay out of the way. Mind if I hang out here for a while until they're finished?"

"No problem, Fred the Fireman. I'll shut off the TV." He turned off the baseball game.

"So can I get you anything? Water? Perhaps a drink?"

Fred shook his head. "No thanks, young man. Much obliged."

Alex nodded. Neither of them spoke for several seconds.

"What brings you to our quaint little building?" Alex asked, finally breaking the silence. "I hope you're ready to be inundated with activities. We love to stay busy around here."

"Indeed I am," Fred answered. "In fact, I'm more than willing to do my part. The days and nights get long at work, so it's nice to get away from that and do other constructive things. I particularly like carpentry work. Since I grew up with lots of tradesmen in the family you learn to do many different things."

"Yeah, I know what you mean," Alex remarked. "I'm from Indianapolis. My father owned a contracting business there and I used to work for him. After I went to college I decided to not go into the family business. My dad was disappointed, but I felt it was important for me to do my own thing.

"Who runs the business now?" Fred asked.

"My older brothers. I felt better about leaving with them around, so I moved out here and have been here ever since.

"You like it here?"

"Well, it's ok. Been here fifteen years now. I like it most of the time. Other times I don't. Indy was big, but nothing like this. But I've got a good job here and decent retirement and benefits, so I don't mind, really."

"What line of work are you in?" Fred asked.

"Insurance regulation. I work for the State. Not the most exciting gig in the world, but it'll do - especially in a recession and all."

Alex was quiet; Fred sat and smiled patiently. "Sometimes I think about going back home, but when I go to visit I remember why I left. Interesting how we romanticize our childhood days, eh?"

"Why yes, I suppose so," Fred remarked. He sat on Alex's leather couch, arms folded with his left hand slowly stroking his silver beard totally engrossed in the conversation. Alex eventually shared a few of his life experiences, telling Fred had been engaged, but Mia, his fiancée, broke it off because she thought he drank too much. She offered to get him help, but he refused, so she made her decision - as difficult as it was. On the day she told him it was over he became so despondent that he nearly drank himself to death.

Alex suddenly stopped, realizing he'd been dominating the conversation.

"Hey, you're the new guy here and I'm doing all the talking," Alex apologized.

"No problem Sonny, I like to listen. Just think of me as ….well…..your Guardian Angel," Fred replied. Alex shook his head when Fred called him 'Sonny'. That's what his mother used to call him as a child.

"I can't help but think this is a deep regret of yours, the fact that you blew it with your girlfriend."

"Yeah you're right," Alex answered glumly. "I really wish I could make it up to her."

"What if I gave you what you asked for - you know, a second chance to put things back in perspective? Would you take it?"

Alex looked at Fred as if he were crazy, though the look on Fred's face indicated he wasn't kidding.

"Would I take it?" Alex repeated, still stunned by Fred's comment. "Well, yeah but I doubt if you could help me."

Alex suddenly began to feel warm. He checked the air conditioner; it was working.

"Well, if I could, would you be willing to take that chance?"

Alex shook his head. "Sure, sure I'd do it," he chuckled, still not knowing where this was going. He wiped his forehead; the heat in his apartment was rising.

"Ok, done deal. But before I grant your wish, first things first," Fred says, checking his watch. "It's almost ten twenty-four, and you have a decision to make. I suggest you make it now."

Alex looked at him funny. The room was terribly hot, but Fred hadn't broken a sweat. "Fred, it's only eight-fifteen. Are you alright?"

"There isn't much time. It's almost ten twenty-four and you've got a decision to make! Please make it now!"

The heat was really getting to Alex. Right after he stood his easy chair exploded in a ball of fire. He stepped back in shock as the fire spread around his living room as if someone were using a flame-thrower. He tried to get out, but the fire blocked the front door. Fred ran after him, grabbed his shoulders tightly.

"Listen, it's almost ten twenty-four and you must make a decision. Please make it now!"

Alex was totally confused by what was happening around him, as a loud piercing sound suddenly went off.

"What must I decide?" he screamed at Fred.

Fred looked directly into his eyes.

"To wake up!"

Alex shook himself upright. His apartment wasn't on fire at all, and Fred was nowhere to be found. He'd passed out in a drunken stupor and the piercing sound he heard was the smoke alarm in the kitchen. He stumbled up from his chair, knocking over the near empty bottle of Jameson's on the floor and ran into the kitchen where he'd left his baked beans on the stove.

Alex made it just in time to see the pot suddenly catch fire. He grabbed an extinguisher on the wall and put out the flames. Once they were finally out, he opened the window above the sink, then stood on a step stool and removed the battery from the smoke alarm. A huge sigh of relief heaved from the center of his chest.

Alex wobbled back to the living room, still a bit unsteady from yet another night of drinking. He wiped his brow, relieved that he'd awakened in time and flopped back into his easy chair. The

77

baseball game was over, and the time on his Westminster clock said exactly ten twenty-four!

The decision had been made. He called Mia and left her a message, promising to beat his alcoholism, begging for her help; a first step on a long road to recovery. He put down his phone, looked up and said: *Thank you Fred, my Guardian Angel, wherever you are!*

Communiqué

By Ulysses Candelario

***

"It is better to have loved and lost than never to have loved at all."
~ Alfred Lord Tennyson

I've always loved poetry. Both of my parents were English teachers and used to read poetry to me as a child. By the age of thirteen I'd already read books by Langston Hughes, Emily Dickinson, Robert Frost, Gwendolyn Brooks and Walt Whitman. When I turned eighteen I'd written my first book of poetry, which I managed to publish five years later. This was quite an accomplishment for someone my age, but the love was so deep that it seemed the words flowed so easily. To me, poetry speaks in ways that only the inner being can understand. I become the written word, and it's through these words that I live my life.

I'm a life member of the Academy of American Poets, winner of the T. S. Eliot Citation of Honor, and recently was selected as United States poet Laureate in 2004. I've sold hundreds of thousands of copies of my books across the world, and my work appears in a variety of textbooks, anthologies and magazines like the New Yorker and the American Poetry Review. All these accomplishments and more I've garnered over the course of my fifty-one years on this earth, and as I re-read these words by Alfred Lord Tennyson a second time, my eyes welled up with tears.

"It is better to have loved and lost than never to have loved at all."

***

Even the profound words of Tennyson, an English poet widely considered the Ambassador of the Victorian Age in poetry, cannot comfort me in my time of sorrow. My hands were shaking as I dropped the card on my living room floor. I began crying for the fifth time today as I read yet another note of sympathy for the death of my life partner Robert, who was taken away from me by an unknown intruder. I used to admire this quote by Tennyson, but now my heart was full of anger and bitterness towards him and everyone for their clichéd notes of sympathy, but then again I recalled the two of us making similar statements to our friends who'd lost someone close. Did I have any right to be so harsh, so judgmental? Perhaps not, and under different circumstances I probably wouldn't say such mean-spirited things. I hope my one true love understands my grief and forgives my actions.

Robert and I lived together in the Old Town section of Alexandria, Virginia for nearly thirty years. We made it a point to get to know all of our neighbors, many of whom were over to our home for cookouts during the summer. We had even invited several of the unmarried residents to share Thanksgiving and Christmas dinners with us. Robert never wanted anyone to be alone for the holidays, and always made it a point to be a considerate host for our guests. He was much better at that stuff than I was, I suppose. I was the one who was difficult to live with, constantly being the nag and demanding of people. Somehow he kept me stable, not allowing me to get too out of control. I secretly admired the fact that he was such a patient man.

"Patience makes lighter what sorrow may not heal," Robert used to say, quoting Horace.

Though he died two weeks ago today, his murder is still so fresh in my mind. An intruder had strangled him to death in our own home while I was away. By the time I arrived the house had been ransacked, and Robert was sprawled out across the living room floor, his face twisted in fear. My loving partner was gone, so undeserving of his fate since he lived his life doing what he loved to do best – helping those in need. Though that was the one thing I loved about him most, how could I ever imagine someone would be so cruel to take the life of such a kind and generous man? What hurt me even more was the fact that he died on September 9th - the date of our thirtieth anniversary.

80

I remember the day we first met, back in 1975. I was a senior at Georgetown University in Washington, taking an English Literature elective on William Shakespeare. As usual I'd arrived late for class. To be honest, I found the instructor boring and tedious as I did all of my professors. Somehow through all my hurrying I'd lost my textbook and heard someone pushing a desk next to mine. I turned to my right and saw a handsome young man who slid their book over to me, offering to share.

"Here, you and I can look on together," he whispered, precious gray eyes shining brightly at me.

"Thank you," I said, smiling back at him, extending my hand in friendship. "My name is Wilson Tudor."

"A pleasure to meet you Wilson. I am Robert Fane. Welcome to the world of William Shakespeare."

"What a nice looking fellow he is," I remember thinking.

He had such a kind demeanor, one that I would grow very fond of as we continued to get to know one another. Fortunately for me we fell in love, and instead of returning home to San Francisco, I decided to stay with Robert after graduation. He was working towards his PhD, wanting to become an English professor and I was close to publishing my personal collection of poetry, which he absolutely insisted I complete.

The first few years were tough, but once my work began to catch on we were able to afford many of the finer things in life, like the house that overlooks the Potomac River in Old Town, and our vacation home along the coast of Maine, near Ogunquit. Robert became my editor and business partner instead of pursuing his own dreams. He never complained, and quite frankly I think he preferred working with me instead. No matter whether I was receiving an award or doing a public speaking event at some university around the world, Robert was right there doing all the "behind the scenes" work for me. Nothing happened unless it had his approval, and I had complete faith that our affairs were well in hand.

Indeed, in his hands, they were.

And now the love of my life was gone forever.

I opened another sympathy card, which read: *"When he shall die, take him and cut him out in little stars, and he will make the face of heaven so fine that all the world will be in love with night and pay no worship to the garish sun."*

These words, written by William Shakespeare from Romeo and Juliet, caused me to cry. I believe this was the sixth time today.

***

Another week passed, then yet another. I'd spent so much time trying to get myself together, but nothing could fill the deep void I felt within my heart. Many family members, including my two brothers, George and Anthony, and my sister Justine, tried to offer their condolences in the best way they could. Robert's brother Jackson also did his best to comfort me, but to no avail.

There is nothing more painful than losing someone you love – there is no substitute for it, no matter how many times you try. God knows I've given it my best shot, for I'm in the middle of trying to complete my seventeenth book of poems, but I haven't been able to come up with a single line – not one stanza – in almost a month. Friends and family alike have tried to tell me that I should put work to the side for now and grieve, but I know my Robert! He'd kick my ass if I ever stopped living my passion.

"Everyone should live their passion! That's what keeps us going! That's what keeps us human!"

There were no truer words ever spoken.

For years I had the same habits when I would come up with ideas to write about. I always carried with me a recording device that I used in case something came to mind. Robert actually was the one who started me on that many years ago. He got tired of me losing pages from my ratty notebooks and told me to *"get with the Twentieth Century before it became the Twenty-First."* I took his suggestion, so for many years I've carried a tape recorder with me in my briefcase. It never left my side.

As technology advanced he eventually switched me to micro cassettes, which are so much easier to use. In fact, as a gift for our twenty-ninth anniversary he took me to Best Buy and bought me a rather nifty one – some Sony product I think - along with a box of twenty-four cassettes. He told me it was either that or a digital voice recorder, but he didn't think I was quite ready for such a high tech gadget. He was right, you know. I tend to like what I like, and that's about it. I'm as slow as it comes to keeping up with current events.

I've tried to come up with ideas, using all the usual influences. I'd take walks along the river, around the Mall in Washington, through the FDR Memorial. Today I decided to take a drive out to Ft. Belvoir and sit on a park bench. It was a beautiful Saturday morning as the leaves were just starting to turn, and I thought the foliage might provide some solace, if not inspiration.

Feeling the gentle breeze flowing in from the Potomac River, I watched groups of people, young and old, walk by on their way to the adventures of the day. Nothing of what I saw or felt could open my mind because of the deep hole in my heart. Instead of speaking profound words filled with splendor and wisdom, all I could do was cry into the microphone of the recorder – spilling my guts to Robert, who was unable to hear the sorrow in my voice. The pain of his loss had become almost unbearable, as if I had a malignant tumor pressing against the base of my skull.

As I sat on the park bench, looking across the river at the majestic skyline of our nation's Capitol, my vision once again became clouded with my own tears. I'd lost count how many times I'd cried since he's been gone, but it was the first time today.

I decided to talk to Robert again, using my recorder. I hadn't "spoken" to him since last night, and though I know he can't hear me I think the act of opening my heart to him through this mechanical device was helping. At least I wasn't quite the sobbing mess like I was a few weeks earlier.

As I reached for my recorder I thought about last night, the fourth Friday in a row of being alone in our home.

Normally on Friday nights Robert and I would sit together on the couch, order a large pizza from Antonio's and throw back a few cocktails, enjoying each other's company. I had my usual Maker's Mark with a splash of ginger ale – very boring and humdrum some would say, but that's me. I've always been rather predictable. Robert was much more adventurous than me; he would choose flashier drinks like Long Island Iced Teas, Sex on the Beach or his favorite – Margaritas with Cuervo Gold, sometimes on the rocks and other times frozen, depending upon his mood.

Always the queen bee of the house, he was so good at putting people at ease, and he was quite the magician at getting me to loosen me up from being the stiff bore I'd always been. After a few cocktails we blasted classic jazz in our den and danced around the room together until we either crapped out and went to bed or spent the remainder of the evening making passionate love to one another on our leather couch.

No matter how old we got, nor how long we'd been together, Robert and I spent many nights as if we were a newlywed couple, and as much as I was a "fuddy-duddy" of sorts, I always came alive when expressing my love for him. He brought that sort of thing out of me, and that same magic translated into my work. He was truly my muse that brought out the best in me.

My memories flashed back to Thursday evening, when I sat watching the Nationals play the New York Mets on television, the final game of the regular season. Robert and I bought season tickets when baseball returned to Washington. Despite some differences we were both big fans of the sport. He remembered the days of the Washington Senators and used to go to games with his dad and brother when they were kids. A native of the Bay Area, my family used to go to A's games together, and whenever Robert and I visited Oakland during the season we'd always take in a game together. Though not a homegrown A's fan, Robert always wore Athletics paraphernalia to the games because I did, and rooted for the team because of me. That was just like him to do so.

Now my evenings were spent in solitude. I didn't call anyone, nor did I answer the phone. Last night in particular was harder than usual, probably because the Nationals ended their year. Just the thought of us beginning the season going to as many games as possible was probably what made this so difficult. Afterward I spent an hour drinking and talking into the microphone, telling Robert how hard life was without him and the horror I felt being the one who found his mangled body. I think I talked more about that than anything.

The soothing sounds of the Potomac River were not enough to comfort me. Recorder in hand I felt the need to open up once again.

I accidentally pressed the play button instead of record. That's when I heard static, as if I searching for a radio station.

"….Hel…..my……..lit….Wil…."

"That's strange. I must've accidentally recorded over my own voice."

I was about to record over the noise when I heard something odd, something that caught my attention.

"Sorr…..you……d…ee….ike…..at…"

I stopped the tape and rewound it, this time taking an earpiece out of my shirt pocket and placing it into the recorder. I turned up the volume, my right hand pressing the earpiece into my right ear. My attention was focused on hearing the words behind the static.

"Hello……my……..Will…..sorry……had…..ee….ike…..at…"

I looked at the recorder and noticed it had a noise reduction switch on the side. I rewound the tape and I listened again.

"Hello my sweet little Willie! Sorry you had to see me like that! I hope you're alright!"

I screamed and snatched the earpiece out of my ear, throwing the recorder to the ground. I got up from the bench, stumbling away as if a madman wielding a knife had risen up behind

84

the bench. But the only madman here at Ft. Belvoir was me. I'd heard something on that tape that made no sense – no sense at all!

I heard the voice of my deceased partner Robert.

That couldn't be possible. How on earth could Robert be contacting me through a micro cassette recorder?   But he was the only one who ever called me *"sweet little Willie,"* so it had to be him. How? And why?

I looked around me; fortunately I was alone. No one saw me freak out as if I'd just awakened from a bad dream, but to be truthful I began to wonder if I had fallen asleep at some point. There's no way Robert's voice should be on that recorder. It wasn't possible.

"I must've fallen asleep," I said aloud. "That's what happened! How could I be so silly and think it was actually Robert's voice?"

I started to laugh in a weak attempt to convince myself this was all wishful thinking. I picked up my recorder and rewound it again, placing the earpiece into my ear a second time.

Listening calmly, what I heard was indeed a surprise.

"Hello my sweet little Willie! Sorry you had to see me like that! I hope you're alright! I just wanted you to know that I love you so much, and wish you were with me because it's so beautiful here. But once I heard you crying out to me I had to make sure you were okay."

The static ended, as did Robert's voice. Only silence played. I listened to his message over and over.

Tears rolled down my face. I couldn't believe I was hearing this, and was convinced I must be losing my mind. Even in death Robert was still professing his love for me. I think it was then I realized how much of a mess I'd become since he'd been gone.

I rewound the tape and began to speak to him.

"Robert, I don't know if I'm losing my mind or not, but I could swear I just heard your voice on this machine. I don't know if that's possible, but if it is – I want you to know I truly miss you more than I've ever missed anyone in my life. I'm sorry that I wasn't there to protect you."

I stopped recording to replay the message. As before, instead of my voice I heard his once again, accompanied by static.

"You're not losing your mind Willie. It's really me. I know you miss me, and I want to help you get through your anguish as best I can. Not to worry about protecting me. You were by my side during thirty wonderful years, and I couldn't have asked for a better guardian."

85

As before, the static ended.

***

For the remainder of that afternoon and the following week I kept the recorder by my side wherever I went, leaving messages that Robert answered, though briefly. Wherever I went, whether to the grocery store, out to dinner at Copeland's Restaurant in Arlington, having cocktails in the den, listening to Miles Davis while taking an evening drive – I made recordings to my wonderful Robert. It was the next best thing to him actually being here, only he wasn't. The more I spoke to him, the more I missed him.

Instead of getting better, I was actually getting worse.

Over time I began to notice a pattern regarding our conversations. After nearly two weeks of speaking to him through this recorder I found Robert only answered things I said to him directly. It was as if these messages were pre-recorded rather than spontaneous. He never volunteered anything on his own. He never said what he was feeling or thinking, nor did he talk about what life was like on the "other side." All he did was listen to my childish babbling and return a simple answer – nothing more, nothing less.

I wanted to know more. I wanted to hear something from Robert instead of making this all about me. In a moment of euphoria I grabbed my recorder intending to do some of the listening for a change. In a way it caused me to chuckle because how do you ask someone that's dead how their day went? What does one say?

"Gee Robert - how's it going in the afterlife? What's up with the 'Big G' these days? Does he ever take a vacation from being in dominion of the earth and heavens?"

I laughed out loud, for I'd gone completely mad.

I grabbed the recorder and pressed the red button to record.

"Hello Robert. I know this may seem like a silly question to you, but for the past few weeks all I've done is talk about me. Sorry about that sweetheart, but it wasn't intentional. I don't have anyone here to talk to, and I'm getting rather lonely. I finally noticed that throughout all of this you've never offered anything about yourself and I wanted to know how come?

I rewound the tape and pressed play, hearing the 'hissing' of the static.

"HAHAHAHAHA," Robert laughed loudly. God, how I missed that laugh of his!

86

"It took a while, but finally I got the million dollar question! Well my dear Sweet Willie, allow me to provide an answer to your nagging conundrum of the day!"

Here we go! I pressed my finger against the earpiece so I wouldn't miss a word.

"The reason I've not offered anything about myself is simply because I can't speak about something which you cannot possibly understand. The after-life is such a wonderful place; a place where dreams are made and the greatest wonders of man are answered. If I were to try to explain it to you, you would never understand me. Let me put it this way – me trying to tell you about life beyond your existence will make as much sense as someone trying to tell a joke outside of the context of the moment. As the expression goes – you'd have to be there to understand."

As always when Robert was finished, the static ended.

"So if I can't understand what you are experiencing presently, can I understand or ask anything from your past life."

I pressed play.

"Now you're catching on! Yes, you may ask me anything you wish. I promise I will answer you truthfully, but please remember to be careful what you ask for. What you hear may be startling. Oh – I can only answer what you ask, so make your questions good."

This caused me to shudder. I think he knew what I was going to ask, and quite frankly I didn't know if I wanted to hear the answer.

I stepped away from the recorder and poured myself a glass of Maker's Mark on the rocks; the warmth of the alcohol coated my parched throat. I closed my eyes and took a deep breath.

Was I sure I wanted to do this? What if I heard something that I couldn't handle?

I pounded down the remnants of the glass until the ice cubes 'clinked' together, and set the glass on the coffee table. It was now or never, and I was ready.

I grabbed the recorder and began to speak.

"What happened when you were attacked? It's not a question I want to ask, Robert, but I have to know. Please tell me."

I stopped the tape. My heart was pounding as if I'd just finished a marathon, but I didn't care. This was the beginning of putting this all behind me.

I pressed play.

"I was in the process of making dinner before you came home from Georgetown, when I saw a tall, bearded man I knew from the neighborhood waving at me through the kitchen window from the sidewalk. I went outside and spoke to him, and as we talked he said he was hungry, so I offered him a sandwich, which I brought to him outside on the front porch. We chatted for the better part of an hour, when he propositioned me. He became agitated when I told him I was not interested and asked him to leave. That's when he attacked me, forcing me back into the living room. I fought him off for as long as I could, but he was too much for me. He strangled me in the living room. Everything went black, and the next thing I knew you were standing over me – crying as I've never seen you cry before."

Robert paused; I could still hear the static. It took all I could for me not to burst out in tears. The memory of finding him was almost too painful to bear, especially a second time. Robert continued to speak:

"Willie, I'm sorry I won't be there for you as I once was. It's wonderful being here, but even in death, our love is as strong as it's always been. I cannot leave you until I know you can move forward with life.....until we meet one another again someday. I cannot go, I can't....can't....."

The static ended, but my crying had only begun. I spent the next hour sprawled out across my leather couch with a seemingly endless stream of tears running down my face, thinking that Robert died while once again trying to do what came natural to him.

I could not save him. The romantic evenings, times taking care of him when he was ill, consoling him when his parents found out about us – all these things meant nothing in the end. He died horrifically. He died alone.

For the first time in my life I'd actually thought of suicide. I couldn't bear the guilt anymore, and I honestly began considering how I would carry out the deed.

That's when I heard my front doorbell ring.

***

I tried to make myself presentable and stood too fast, given the fair amount of hits from bottle of Maker's Mark, extending my arms outward to keep from falling over as I stumbled towards the front of the house.

The doorbell continued ringing; obviously the person was desperately awaiting my arrival. I made it to the front door and looked through the peephole. There was a tall, bearded man,

88

probably in his thirties, wearing a camouflage jacket with a jungle-green t-shirt underneath. The man had a grungy look, his face clearly was dirty and there were rips around the collar of his shirt, as well as on his jacket.

The doorbell caused my head to throb. I definitely had had too much to drink.

"Who are you and why are you ringing my bell like a madman?"

"Sorry – I was looking for Robert, is he home?"

Whoever this was, he obviously hasn't been here in some time.

"Robert is dead, my friend. He's been dead for over a month, now please – leave me alone."

I watched the man's reaction. His face seemed to harden, as I could see his gray-colored eyes bug out and his jaw tighten. The stranger began pounding on the door, and judging by the force of his blows he obviously was quite strong.

"Open this fucking door! You are in grave danger, sir – just like your partner was! Open it or I will break it down!"

I grabbed a phone and dialed 911, screaming into the receiver that a crazy person was beating on my door. Within two minutes a squad car pulled up, and despite the fact that the police showed, the man continued to scream at the top of his lungs, demanding to be let in.

Through my front window I witnessed a City of Alexandria police officer take down the stranger, though it wasn't easy. The officer finally wrestled him to the ground, placed him in handcuffs and escorted the stranger to the back of the police car. When I felt safe enough, I opened my door and stepped out onto the front porch.

Officer Simon Jackson approached the house. He was the same officer that arrived when I called about Robert's attack. He was a tall, well-built man with a neatly trimmed beard, and just like last time he wore a crisp navy-blue uniform, which fit his muscular frame like a glove. Officer Jackson looked like he could start as a defensive back for the Raiders.

"Hello, Mr. Tudor. I'm sorry to see you again under such circumstances."

He extended his hand. As I shook it, my own hand was completely swallowed by his; the tightness of his grip had registered a mild jolt that shot straight up my arm. I could only imagine what it felt like being on the receiving end of his fist when it was thrown in anger or self-defense.   The officer smiled as he released his grip, his eyes concealed by dark sunglasses and the brim of his hat. Come to think of it, he wore sunglasses the last time I saw him too.

"No problem, Officer – I'm glad you're here. Who the hell is this lunatic and what did he want with Robert?"

That seemed to pique the officer's interest.

"He mentioned your partner? What did he say?"

"I told him that Robert was dead and he refused to believe me. He said I was in danger and threatened to break down the door. That's it, really - except……..."

"Except what?" The officer took out a pad and began taking notes.

"Well – I've never seen this man before, but he obviously knew Robert was gay. I think he also was aware I lived here and knew I wasn't him. Strange that Robert never mentioned this man to me. Do you know him?"

The officer nodded. "Name's John Davis - a burnout drifter and former Green Beret who served in the Gulf War. Never came back to reality after returning home. Hits the bottle early and often, and has been picked up for disorderly conduct, trespassing and the like. It's not the first time he's been here, either. I've stopped by before when John was bothering your partner."

"I wonder why Robert never told me about this man. That wasn't like him to do that."

"Well, I imagine he didn't want to worry you about it. John begged for food and money, and since Robert would give it to him, the guy would disappear for a while, only to suddenly show up again later. He stopped coming around when I threatened to arrest him the last time I was here, but I guess he's back up to his old tricks again."

"Well I'd appreciate it if you could keep him from coming around again. I don't like the idea of some vagabond pounding on my front door. "

"I'll do what I can, Mr. Tudor, but just in case – here's my card. Call me at the station if you need anything. And again, I'm sorry about your loss."

I thanked the officer, my hand vanishing as he shook it a second time. I watched as the squad car disappeared down the street with John Davis staring at me from the rear window.

I went to the den, needing to know why Robert never told me about John.

I began speaking into the recorder, my voice slightly agitated.

90

"Robert – how come you never told me about John Davis? He was just here pounding on the front door like he was completely out of his mind, demanding to see you. I called the police and Officer Jackson was the one who told me about him."

I listened to the tape. The static began.

"Willie – I'm sorry I never said anything about John, but it was for your own protection. If John shows up again just do what he wants and he'll go away."

The message was over.

This was getting ridiculous. Why on earth would Robert not want me to call the police? I HAD to know why.

"Robert, you're not making sense. Why the hell shouldn't I call the police to keep this creep away from our house? Not calling could be dangerous!"

Static began again.

"Because John might come back and kill you as he did me!"

A chill ran down my spine. Robert had shared with me the identity of his murderer – who had just been at my house! The vagabond that came to my door demanding to be let in took the life of my partner.

I rewound the tape to leave another message.

"Robert, why on earth would this man murder you if you've been giving him what he wanted? I can understand he's a little psycho, but Officer Jackson said he'd usually leave if you fed him. Help me out here, because I'm confused. There must be something I'm missing."

I waited for his response.

"Willie, you don't understand! John is……"

SNAP!

The tape in the recorder had broken. After working on it I managed to eject the cassette, and carefully unraveled the residue. From there I spent the better part of the afternoon trying to splice the tape, eventually doing so successfully, then snapped the shell back together.

I placed the cassette back in the recorder and left a message.

"Robert, can you repeat your last answer? I didn't hear all of it!"

There was no static. In fact, all I heard were a series of messages I'd left to my deceased partner over the past few weeks. There were no responses from him at all.

91

I tried to leave another message, but it didn't work no matter how hard I tried. I even went to the store and purchased a new tape, thinking that would be the answer, but it wasn't. I was now left with a new reality that I didn't want to think possible. There was no coming back on this one.

I'd lost Robert forever.

***

It was near the middle of November, over two months from Robert's death. As the temperatures had dwindled so had my ability to work. I was closing in on the deadline for my next book and I hadn't written anything in quite a while. I felt as if I had no outlet whatsoever – ever since that damned tape had broken. I often spent time walking through the house, pondering the last part of my conversation that had been cut off.

"Willie, you don't understand! John is......"

What was Robert trying to tell me about John? On this rainy Wednesday afternoon I looked outside and noticed John was gone, which was strange. Since Officer Jackson arrested him I've seen him on numerous occasions watching over my house, staring at me as if he were waiting for something, biding his time for the right moment to attack. Because Robert said so, I didn't call the police, afraid of what would happen if I did. I felt fine knowing I could see his position, but now that he was gone I became worried.

John, what are you up to?

Officer Jackson called once shortly after he was here to let me know that John had been released, asking had I seen or heard from him. Of course I told him no, and in all honesty what exactly could the police do about the matter? Technically John hadn't done anything that could get him arrested; he wasn't on my property and all he did was stand there, acting more like a watchdog than someone I should be concerned about. As long as he didn't come too close I'd just have to deal with it.

I decided to clear out some of Robert's closets and for the last week or two I'd considered the possibility of selling the house. I couldn't care for it as well as he had. Robert kept this place together so well, and I didn't understand how that was possible since I was so busy working long hours in my upstairs office. For the most part, while working he knew to leave me to my thoughts. Every now and then, he'd come upstairs during lunchtime with sandwiches and juice and we'd eat together – then he'd go back to what he was doing somewhere in the house. Sometimes though,

92

he'd surprise me by coming to my office wearing only his black silk robe, telling me *he* was on the lunch menu for the day.

Oh how I missed those days!

I smiled as I held Robert's robe, reminiscing over the days I spent watching him walk across a room with it on, and thinking how excited I would be in taking it off of him.

No matter how good a lover someone else might be for me, no one would ever compare. As the song says – *"long as we live, you will always be my first."* I smelled the robe; a faint trace of my first and only love still graced the material. I smiled and returned the robe to its rightful place in his closet. I'd never get rid of it – no matter what.

Robert had a lot of items neatly packed in boxes in his closet. Each box was labeled in black marker on its side: books, personal information, clothes, etc. I took a look through each box, deciding to keep much of what was there. He was good at removing junk from our shelves and storage spaces. I couldn't help but think Robert probably did this so he could make it easier for me in case he passed away before I did. It was just like him to think so far ahead.

As I came to a box labeled *"Wilson Miscellaneous"*, I found a plastic bag that said "Best Buy" and inside was an unopened box of twenty-four tapes and a receipt. That's when I remembered that the tape I originally had in the recorder also was purchased that same day. I'd never changed the tape.

According to the receipt, the recorder and tapes were bought on September 9th, 2004, the date of our anniversary, at approximately 1:48pm. My eyes opened wide in shock, and with good reason. That was the exact time I found Robert dead on our living room floor one year later!

"This is the link!" I shouted.

I ran downstairs full speed with the bag of tapes and searched the den for my recorder. I ripped open the bag, tapes flew everywhere, and was about to put one into the recorder when I heard a sound behind me. Before I could turn around someone had grabbed me from behind and covered my mouth; their left hand wielded one of my knives from the kitchen. I tried to scream, but the right hand of my attacker tightened on my mouth.

"Shhhhhhhhhhhhhhhhhhh……….keep quiet Mr. Tudor!"

Even though the person was whispering I knew it was John. I felt this was it! First he murdered my partner, now he's come back for me! The thing I still couldn't understand is why. Why would he kill us both? Did he hate gays? Did he want to rob us of house and home? Or was this merely some act of a crazy and deranged man? I had no idea, but I truly believed I was about to die.

John put his lips to my left ear and began to whisper: "Don't scream, Mr. Tudor or else I will cut you! Do you understand?"

I nodded, fearing for my life.

"I just wanted to let you know that I'm watching every move you make. It's for your own protection, in case the enemy decides to attack you! We can't have these assholes doing what they wish anymore. We're going to be tough and ready for action. You are to call no one, you are to tell no one what is going on. We will sit quietly and go about our business as if nothing is happening until they decide to attack, do you understand?"

I nodded again. This man was out of his mind. He sounded as if he were still on the battlefield of some long-ago war.

"Remember – I'm watching you, so tell NO ONE! You will sit down, turn on the television and wait for one minute before getting up."

I felt John release his tight grip, then I sat down as I was told, hearing his footsteps become faint behind me. I was shaking so violently I thought I would explode. My eyes focused on the digital clock on my DVD player, and when one minute passed I looked around me – the sound of heavy rain outside came from the kitchen. The side door to the house was open, so I locked it and stared hard at the phone on the wall. I know he said to not call anyone, but if I didn't I was afraid he'd freak out again and kill me next time.

I couldn't wait. I had to do it!

I dialed the Alexandria Police Department. Someone answered the phone.

"Police department, how can I help you?"

I whispered into the receiver. "Yes, my name is Wilson Tudor. I'm looking for Officer Simon Jackson. Please tell him it's an emergency – someone's just broken into my home."

"Hold on sir, let me see if he's on duty this afternoon."

I heard the operator put the receiver on her desk. The sound of people and noise and ringing telephones in the background blared into my ear. I also heard someone ask if 'Johnny' was on duty this afternoon, to which there was a muffled response. Not too long after that the operator came back onto the phone.

"Hello sir, Officer Jackson is on duty today, but he's not in the station. Would you like me to dispatch him to your address?"

"Yes ma'am, tell him to come to Wilson Tudor's house on North Union Street. I'll be waiting for him."

"OK sir, I'll do that for you right now!"

I hung up the phone and walked carefully back into the den. Fortunately I didn't hear or see any sign of John.

That's when it hit me!

I ran back into the kitchen and called the police department again. The same voice answered as before.

"Ma'am, excuse me but this is Mr. Tudor again. I couldn't help but overhear someone ask if 'Johnny' was on duty this afternoon. Who is this 'Johnny'?"

The operator grumbled as if I'd asked a dumb question.

"'Johnny' is Officer Jackson! He goes by his middle name, John. I've already notified him that you called, and he said he's on his way, Mr. Tudor."

I hung up the phone without answering her and bolted into the den. I grabbed one of the cassette's I'd spilled on the floor and quickly jammed it into the recorder, pressing the red button.

"Robert! Please tell me you can hear me! I've figured out that there are TWO men named John, and one of them is on his way here. I must know which John attacked you! PLEASE TELL ME!"

I looked out my window noting the storm was picking up in intensity, and I rewound the tape – praying that Robert would answer.

I began to hear the same static as before.

"Willie you must get out of that house before John gets there. The 'John' that attacked me was the police officer! Get out before it's too late! GET OUT NOW, WILLIE!"

I dropped the recorder and ran for the front porch, only to find Officer Jackson waiting as I opened the door.

***

"Hi Mr. Tudor. I came just as soon as I could. Are you alright?" the Officer asked.

I stood there speechless, too afraid to move an inch. I thought I might pass out.

"Mr. Tudor, what's wrong? Here – why don't you sit down. You look totally freaked out!"

He came into the house and shut the door behind him. He took me by the arm and brought me into the living room, gesturing me to sit. He reached out to me and caressed my cheek with his meaty hand.

95

"You poor thing! You appear to have had quite a shock. Let me take a look around and make sure the house is clear. Afterward I'll make you a drink-- Maker's Mark, right?"

I gave a weak nod as he began searching the house. A few minutes later he brought me a glass of Maker's Mark on the rocks and set it down next to me before making his way upstairs. For once, alcohol was the last thing on my mind.

I didn't know what to do. My better sense told me to get up and run, but I was afraid of what would happen if he caught me. No matter what I did, I knew he'd find me. It would be best if I didn't do anything until he left. I'd figure out what my next move was from there.

I heard the staircase creak as he came down, but he was no longer dressed in his officer's uniform. Instead he was wearing Robert's silk robe and appeared to be completely nude under it. Sitting next to me on the couch and removing the robe, his naked body on full display, he began to gently rub my back. I've never in my life wanted to scream more than I did right now.

"There's no one here, Mr. Tudor. It's just you and me, finally alone together. I figured that call of yours was bogus and you'd eventually come around to seeing things my way."

Flashes of lighting lit up the sky, followed by loud rolls of thunder. The storm was right on top of us, and now no one would hear my screams for help. I kept telling myself 'this couldn't possibly be happening', but indeed it was.

"What are you doing?" I whispered. "What do you want from me?"

"Oh come on now, Willie – may I call you Willie? Please call me John – all my friends do."

This crazy office continued to rub my back. For the first time I could see his hazel colored eyes.

"I've long known who you were and have followed your work. You have been an inspiration to me for years. It took time and money bribing that derelict John Davis to get some information about you, but I had to figure something out. I had to get next to the man who brought me a new lease on life. For so many years I struggled with my sexuality, thinking I'm supposed to act like I'm straight. But your work convinced me to be who I am on the inside, no matter what – and for that I owe you my life. I tried to tell Robert how much I wanted you, but he refused to grant me my wish."

I looked into the eyes of this hulking madman.

96

"What wish was that, John?" I asked, my voice trembling with fright.

The officer opened his mouth to speak again.

"He wouldn't share you with me, so I got rid of him. And since I get what I want, you are all mine. I can make you happy; no one will harm you as long as I'm here, you'd better believe that."

I tried my hardest to fight back tears. This man was a complete psychopath and I'd fallen for it. Robert and John were both right. I never should have called the police.

Officer Jackson closed the distance between him and me, gently leaning me against his broad, muscular shoulders.

"Make love to me Willie, and I'll do everything I can to please you. I promise you that!"

His lips neared mine for a kiss, when suddenly I looked past Officer Jackson's shoulder and saw John Davis standing in the hallway. He motioned for me to be very quiet. He quietly slid behind Officer Jackson and put him in a headlock, dragging him over the back of my couch. I screamed and jumped away from the fracas as John Davis sidestepped and stabbed him in the torso, back and spine. Like the soldier he once was, his attack was quick, clean and effective. The body of Officer Simon John Jackson hit the ground with a huge 'thud' – legs convulsing before slowly coming to a stop.

"Johnny" died on my living room floor, exactly where I had found Robert two months ago.

***

The Alexandria Police Department, an ambulance and a huge crowd of reporters and onlookers were at my home within a half hour. I sat next to John Davis, who'd just finished giving a statement to the police as I tried to grasp everything that happened that day. Robert died because he refused to share me with anyone else; even someone who was physically more powerful than he. Reminded of how my Robert was so selfish, so greedy, and so wonderfully passionate about the people he loved—me more than anyone else--I smiled.

I'd asked John if he would stay, since he'd been the one who graciously saved my life. Though he was a tad high-strung, I knew he wouldn't harm me and I thought he'd appreciate a clean place to stay for a change. He seemed very grateful, and I was glad I could help. I offered him food and shot of whiskey. He took the food, but said he had given up drinking in favor of finding something positive to occupy his time. I was glad he trusted me enough to help him. I guess I'm learning something that Robert had known for so many years – how to help another human being who was in need. I felt better already because of it.

After the police left and things had quieted down, I grabbed the recorder and left Robert another message thanking him for being there for me, as always. His response, of course, was short – but to the point. This time he decided to quote Buddha, and said: *"Let us rise up and be thankful, for if we didn't learn a lot today, at least we learned a little, and if we didn't learn a little, at least we didn't get sick, and if we got sick, at least we didn't die; so, let us all be thankful."*

I laughed.

"Thank you baby – I love you now and forever."

I rewound the tape to listen to his response, but instead of static I heard my own voice. Passage after passage, the most beautiful words I'd ever thought within the deepest realms of my mind had come alive on tape. After listening to nearly ten of the twenty-four cassettes from the torn package I'd come to realize once again Robert was taking care of me. My voice, my expression was back, thanks to him.

In the den I held an old photograph taken of Robert and me, taken on an Alaskan cruise during our twenty-fifth anniversary celebration. I hugged the photo and thanked God for the blessings He'd given me over the years with such a wonderful life partner. Robert could never be replaced, but I also understood that my life will go on, with the belief that someday the two of us will be together again, sharing our special love with one another as it was meant to be. I don't care what anyone says; God brought my Robert to me, and I'll always be grateful for the life that we had together.

And as I looked through my window, watching the rain come down in gentle drops I remember thinking once again about Alfred Lord Tennyson's famous quote:

"It is better to have loved and lost than never to have loved at all."

Thank goodness for love! How sweet it is!

In Timely Fashion
By Ina Austin
***

Part One: "Felix" (Latin for "Happy and Prosperous")

The changing seasons can be bittersweet. Some prefer summer, the perfect time for vacationing, mowing lawns and gardening. Others may prefer the crisp fall breeze with its colored leaves that create picturesque scenes across the plains, or 'prairies' as they are called here in Illinois. There are even a select few who actually enjoy the winter months; heavy snow, grey skies and below zero weather. As for Felix Laszlo, local bus driver and all-around nice guy, his favorite time of the year was always the same: fall, because it meant the start of the school year.

Felix loves children, but unfortunately can't have his own - damn Laszlo genes, as he often called it. Infertility had reared its ugly head in his family before; he was just the most current victim. When his ex-wife found out about his 'problem' their marriage was never the same, and it sadly sputtered to an end shortly thereafter. Felix took their divorce hard, but recently he had come to grips with his situation. It just wasn't in the cards for him to be a father or a husband, he surmised.

Today marked his fifth anniversary as a bus driver for St. William School on Chicago's South Side. Felix enjoyed his job more than anything. He liked seeing the kids' smiling faces in the morning, and often bought treats for them to have with their lunches, though he'd never buy candy. Instead he asked the parents about

99

healthy things he could buy for them, and if they did all their homework he'd give them their treat. Several parents wrote glowing remarks about Felix to the school as the kids were actually motivated to do their homework in part because of his little rewards. Felix would also play music on the bus, but not the popular stuff you hear today. Instead he'd play music from the 1970s and 1980s-- Earth, Wind & Fire, Simply Red and Gloria Estefan were some of his favorites. The kids seemed to have a particular affinity for Cyndi Lauper, so he'd play *Time After Time* on most mornings. By the end of the last school session every child on his bus had learned the entire song, much to Felix' delight.

If there was anything to be said against Felix, it was his lack of punctuality. Last year he was written up twice for being late, and although Felix did his best to remain focused, eventually the stress from his divorce began to take its toll. His boss understood and chose to not put his reprimands in his file, but a talk was necessary, which Felix certainly understood. Once his divorce was final he promised Mr. Caruthers there would be no further problems. This coming year, Felix was intent on keeping his promise.

The first day of school was always the longest, as he made sure he took his time getting to know each new child on his bus and asking his regulars how they spent their summers. Once every child had been accounted for, Felix made his way to Costco to purchase a list of supplies for the principal's office, one of his many tasks during the day. Usually when he was alone he would blast his Cyndi Lauper CD and sing to himself, not caring if he missed a note or flubbed a line because, in his mind, real singing fed the soul. His mother sang on the church choir many years ago, and though she didn't have much of a voice, she always seemed refreshed when she returned from choir practice or a performance. Her choir director was the one who told her that singing feeds the soul. She passed that on to Felix, and since he was unable to have children of his own, he passed that on to the kids on his bus rather than keep it to himself.

Girls Just Wanna Have Fun had ended. *When You Were Mine* was next, but it reminded him too much of his ex-wife, so he skipped over it and went straight for *Time After Time*. Just as he pushed the button, he caught a glimpse of a little girl standing at the corner of Bell Avenue and West 116th street. She wore a uniform similar to kids at school and had long brown hair braided into pigtails with white barrettes at the ends. Strangely enough she was facing away from the street, staring at the white Victorian house on the corner. Felix knew most houses in the neighborhood; this one had belonged to the Williams family, who had recently sold it and moved on to Joliet. No new owners had moved in yet, as far as he knew. He began to panic, thinking he might've missed this little girl on her first day of school.

"I'm such an idiot," he thought, as he slid his bus to the curb. The girl continued to stare at the house. Felix still couldn't see her face.   She was dressed in a checkered green and white jumper dress that came down just below her knees. Her white blouse had ruffles along the collar, and she wore long, white stockings and black penny loafers. From the back her hair appeared neatly groomed and she had white ribbons that tied together her pigtails. Clearly the little girl was dressed for school, but despite his arrival she still hadn't moved an inch.

"Mister Laaaaaszloooooo," she said, in a slow, deliberate manner. Her voice was very deep for a young child.

"Yes?" he replied.

"Be on time tomorrow or I will die."

The girl faced him, and Felix recoiled in fright. Her throat had been cut from ear to ear and her blouse was stained with blood. Instead of boarding, she turned and walked toward the rear of the bus, moving out of Felix's line of sight. He jumped off the bus and searched for her, but she was gone; vanished into thin air.

"Be on time tomorrow or I will die," he whispered quietly to himself.

***

Part Two: "Laszlo"
(Hungarian for "the embodiment of virtue and bravery")

All night Felix was preoccupied with what he'd experienced. It was all so weird. She knew his name and asked him to "be on time or she would die," which he guessed alluded to his past lateness, but how did she know that? How does that explain her throat being slashed open? All that blood on that poor child; was it a warning? He couldn't stop thinking about it. The macabre image ran through his mind like it was on instant replay. He didn't understand her message, but he was determined to be there - just in case.

At seven o'clock sharp Felix carried his steaming mug of coffee and backpack of goodies for the kids to his bus parked in the driveway. He began the morning serenade with Do You Really Want to Hurt Me by Culture Club, followed by Human Nature by Michael

Jackson, a nice precursor to a busy day. Once all the kids were in the bus he'd turn on Time After Time, hand out the treats and listen to them sing. This was the highlight of his day.

Felix decided his last stop would be at Bell Avenue and West 116th Street, and as he approached the corner he saw the little girl from yesterday. Once again she had her back turned to him, and as he pulled over he saw a young woman come out of the house, approaching the bus. The girl turned. No blood, no stains - only smiles. The two of them stared at one another for what seemed like several long minutes. Lazlo looked at the woman, who appeared pleasant and engaging, though mother and daughter hardly resembled one another. Perhaps she looked more like her father, Felix thought. He also wondered if he were "on time."

"Good morning sir. I'm Karen, and this is Ashley. Say hi to the bus driver, honey."

"Hi," Ashley said, raising her right hand. Felix was somewhat nervous, unsure whether or not he had imagined the entire thing yesterday. Better yet, he wondered if this cute but peculiar young girl remembered something about the incident.

"Uh…Hi, Ashley. I'm Mr. Laszlo. I take it you're new in school?"

Ashley nodded.

"We just moved in yesterday," Karen said. "This is her first day."

"Well come aboard Ashley. I'll make sure you get to school on time."

Ashley boarded the bus, waving goodbye to Karen, who turned and headed back toward the old Williams house. Ashley sat behind Felix, and as the kids continued their morning serenade he began to chat with her. As it turned out, Karen was her foster parent and was in the process of adopting her legally. It was clear by the way Ashley was groomed and her good manners that Karen would make a good mother.

Felix pulled the bus into the school parking lot and opened the door for the kids, standing outside wishing everyone a good day. Ashley was the last to leave the bus. She stopped a moment and gestured for Felix to come closer. He knelt down as she whispered in his ear: "Thanks for being on time."

***

Since Felix had some down time he sat in his bus, sipping his coffee and listening to the radio when a police car came into the parking lot. Two uniformed officers went into the school and to Felix'

102

amazement, they came out with Ashley and Mrs. Johnson, the school principal. Felix asked Mrs. Johnson what was wrong as they placed Ashley in the back of their squad car.

"Oh Felix, it's just horrible," Mrs. Johnson said, whispering so Ashley wouldn't hear.

"That poor girl's foster mother was killed by her ex-boyfriend about a half hour ago. He broke into her house and slashed her throat with a knife from her kitchen. The man called the police afterwards, then cut his own wrists and lay down next to her. The police found them together on the kitchen floor."

He spoke briefly to the officers, then looked at Ashley. Something about the look in her eyes told him she knew what was going on. Exactly how she knew was the mystery.

"Ashley, would you like to get some ice cream? The officers have agreed to let you stay with me for a while."

She nodded, opened the door and gently took his hand. And as they began walking to the school cafeteria, Felix began thinking he could get used to this.

"Sweet Serendipity"
By Teresa Rodriguez
***

"Another day has passed, and another begins," I thought, staring at the spinning silhouette of my Venetian ceiling fan.

Since rays of sunlight were beginning to creep through my blinds I knew that it was somewhere around five-thirty in the morning on this soon-to-be hot August day in Chicago. The thought of doing anything outside of my home when the temperature was supposed to reach ninety-five degrees was not appealing in the least, but I had to go to work. Being the sole proprietor of Senora Hermosa Clothiers meant I constantly thought of my business 24/7, and I couldn't afford to take time off right now – not with Rosa, my general manager, being out on a much needed vacation. I guess I didn't realize how important she was until she began her three-week vacation to Mexico a couple of days ago. I now realize she deserves a raise.

I sat up in my half-empty king-sized bed and rubbed my eyes, which felt raw – probably from all the crying I've been doing for the last few weeks, including last night.

Two weeks ago yesterday, after three years of living together, my boyfriend Javier walked out on me. I took a look at his side of the bed and remembered days waking up and seeing him sleeping, watching his chest quietly rise and fall as he breathed with such ease. Many mornings I would wake him with kisses and certain other things, to his delight. I recalled days spent in each other's arms, talking about our plans for building a life together. He and I had known each other since we were kids in grade school. Both of us came from big families and grew up in Pilsen/Little Village, one of the largest Mexican-American communities in Chicago. We were going to get married and start a family.

Everything was in place—at least I thought – until I came home and he told me he didn't want to get married after all. I'd been away on a trip to visit one of my distributors in New York, and upon my return I found him sitting in the living room, his bags packed and all his personal belongings gone. I practically begged him to tell me why he wanted to leave, but he only responded that he wasn't ready for marriage. He never looked me in the eye, never tried to comfort me, and continued to say the same thing over and over again.

"I'm sorry Alma, but I don't want to marry you."

Each time stung worse than before, and I grew so angry that I slapped him with such force that I thought I'd sprained my hand. The last thing I remember doing was opening all of his suitcases and throwing his clothes individually out the front door – telling him to follow that crap to the sidewalk. I had never snapped like that before, but this was such a surprise that I didn't know what to do. I was stunned as he callously walked out my front door without saying a single word.

A couple of times I almost called him, but my mother told me it was best that I didn't. If he wanted to get back together he had to make the first move, not me. She was right, but still it hurt nonetheless. How do you move on when so much of your life was wrapped up in one person?

"Step by step," my mother said to me, the first of hundreds of times during the three-week span. Easier said than done, I say - but in reality what else is one to do? I had no choice but to move on.

After getting dressed, making myself a hot cup of coffee and reading the Chicago Tribune I left my Morgan Park home and drove to Evergreen Plaza Shopping Center on 95th and Western. The Plaza has been a part of the south suburban Evergreen Park community since 1952, and over the years has seen stores come and go, including major retail chains like Montgomery Ward, Woolworth's and Kresge's. It's sad, but all those stores went out of business years ago.

I could remember as a little girl going with my mother to Evergreen Plaza. Even though it was on the far south side, my mother insisted on going because she could do everything she wanted without leaving the mall. She'd buy new clothes for both of us, get her hair and nails done and sometimes take me to the movies or for ice cream. I even remember the days when Games Galore and Orange Julius were the hot spots for kids to go to. Even though those places are now gone, I still take a walk by that section of the lower level and sit on a bench watching the kids go by – thinking they don't know what they missed. I spent so much money in Games Galore on "Pac-Man" and "Dragon's Lair" that my mother would give me extra allowance money so I could play a little longer. For some strange reason that part of the mall still remains empty. No one has leased that space since Games Galore and Orange Julius moved out years ago. Every time I look at that place I find myself reminiscing about the good old days. I even remember going there with Javier. He and I used to go there as kids, and…

"NO! I'm not going to think about him right now! I'm going to go to work and have a productive sales day!" I said aloud, as I entered the Plaza parking lot.

I kept telling myself this over and over again, while listening to the morning news on the radio.

***

My favorite part of coming to work was listening to soft elevator music on the lower level. It was a calming thing for me most mornings. Sometimes I wondered what others thought of this music; no singing, no instruments, just sounds coming from some electronic keyboard. To be honest, at one time I hated it, but now it seemed to put me in a mellow mood as I began each workday, perhaps because there were no words to distract me from my surroundings. It wasn't particularly good music, but it was just enough to allow me to wander on my own for a while, something I needed from time to time. Until, of course, I got some blue-haired old battle-axe trying to haggle over the price of a blouse. Believe it or not, I got one of those almost every day. Different hag, same hair color.

I shook off the temptation to start reminiscing about Javier once again as I reached my storefront. I bent down to unlock the steel gate that closed off the entryway. With a single snatch upward I watched the gate lock into place above my head, then unlocked the door and punched in "051970" to my alarm. That was Javier's birthday, of course. I really need to change that password.

It was nine-fifteen. I expected Crystal to arrive shortly, so I thought I'd help her out and open the register. I felt really blessed to have such a good group of employees, and tried to reward them as best as possible with bonuses and decent time off. Sometimes I'd even let them take a day off, off the books. Every now and then it's important to do the little things to keep your sales staff happy.

A short time later I saw Crystal's smiling face come through the glass doors. She reached down and locked them since we didn't open for another half hour. I immediately noticed that she walked with a certain poise that usually comes from women who are happy about something. That 'something' was usually men, and as I recall she'd met a guy a few months ago here in the mall. I often struggled to remember his name - Dwayne, I think - so instead I referred to him as 'Mr. Wonderful', since that's all she ever called him. But this time she seemed different. There was an inner glow that flowed like an aura through her pores and shined brightly against anything within five feet of her. It's been a while since I'd seen anyone quite like that. Not too long ago I used to be that way. At least I thought I was.

"Good morning, Alma dahhhhling!" Crystal said, with a toothy smile reminding me of the Cheshire cat from "Alice in Wonderland."

"Hello Crystal. I see your date went well last night. And what did Mr. Wonderful do to make you such a love-sick fool this morning?"

Before I could even finish my sentence, she held up her left hand - flashing a beautiful diamond engagement ring and wagging it in my face like Ricki Lake in "Hairspray."

I couldn't believe it! Mr. Wonderful asked this vibrant, young girl to marry him!

"Isn't it beautiful? We went to the White Sox game with our parents last night and he proposed to me when our names appeared on the scoreboard. The camera came on us when I accepted and everyone in Sox Park applauded. Oh Alma, it was so romantic! Imagine it - I am going to be Mrs. Wonderful."

My eyes lowered as I forced a rather weak smile, still too wrapped up in my own nonsense to be overly happy for her. That was my fault. This was a special time for her and I took all the air out of her good fortune.

"Hey - don't worry sweetie. You'll find someone who will treat you special someday. Forget Javier! He isn't worth it."

I nodded, weak smile intact. This was really sad. I should be the one doing the talking right now.

Crystal opened her purse and grabbed a small box from the inside. A replica of Cupid shooting his arrow was embroidered in gold on top of the box. Below the likeness in matching gold cursive print were the words "Sweet Serendipity," and according to the address it was located right here in Evergreen Plaza in the lower level, east wing, where Games Galore and Orange Julius used to be. I'd just walked by there this morning and nothing was there. That had to be a misprint, but even still, the Plaza management would've notified us of a new store opening up.

Crystal opened the box and offered me a piece of chocolate. How could I refuse? Coffee and chocolate at 9:35am? What could be better?

"Well don't just stand there with your mouth open, take a chocolate! I guarantee you, one bite of this and you'll feel better immediately."

I didn't see how I'd feel better by eating a chocolate truffle, but given my present state of affairs it certainly couldn't hurt. I took a piece and bit into it, and immediately my eyes opened wide. Totally ensconced in the rich flavor of the truffle, I felt a rush flow through my body like a jolt of electricity. Crystal was right. A sudden feeling of euphoria came over me, so much that I felt I needed another piece.

"Crystal - this is really good chocolate. In fact, I'd say it's the best piece of chocolate I've ever tasted."

I reached for another one, when Crystal suddenly closed the box.

"Uh uh, only one per customer. Those are the rules!"

Only one per customer? Those were the rules? What the hell was she talking about?

"If you want more you have to go to Sweet Serendipity and get some. The shop owner told me to tell that to anyone I give a candy to. That even goes for bosses!"

She took her purse to the back and started getting ready to open the store. As she disappeared around the corner I licked my fingers, thinking that I would have to take a walk over to Sweet Serendipity and buy a box for myself.

After all, I'm a very sweet person - the sweetest person I know.

***

I took a walk over to the east side of the mall early that afternoon. I must admit that I was still somewhat shocked at the thought of a new store being in that section of the mall. Just the other day I was reminiscing about the good old days of being a kid. For some reason my mind really must've wanted those days back and I'd managed to take myself to another place in time. Whatever

108

the reason, I had a major blackout about the whole thing. It happens, I guess, when love has gone sour.

I casually sang to myself as I walked by the stores, the food court and the atrium where Santa Claus entertains the kids each year during Christmas. Every now and then there is an Easter Bunny on the stage for Easter egg hunts, but that hasn't been as popular lately. My mom always made sure I got there early for the events - even the egg hunts. One time I found an egg that was worth ten dollars in Montgomery Ward. I used it to buy a GI Joe with the kung-fu grip because I went to see "Trading Places" with Eddie Murphy with my cousin Louisa when I was eleven and Eddie had a kung-fu grip, so I absolutely had to have one too! I snickered because I remembered getting Louisa in trouble for taking me to see an R-rated movie. She didn't take me to the movies again until I was an adult. Poor Louisa! Mother was too hard on you!

As I approached the lower level of the east wing I could see red and white balloons on a posted sign that said "Sweet Serendipity – This Way." Oh well! I guess that meant it was official: Games Galore and Orange Julius were finally gone.

Ahead there were more red and white streamers and balloons, plus the sound of music and the luscious aroma of chocolate from around the corner. My eyes opened wide as I stared at a huge neon sign resting above the opening of the store. It was written in red, cursive print saying "Sweet Serendipity" with a likeness of Cupid to the right that fired his arrows towards a heart that was to the left. The store resembled an old fountain shop from the fifties. There were large soda jerks behind the counter, white counter-tops with red stools built into the floor for patrons to sit on. The lounge area had an array of small round tables and skinny chairs with heart shaped backs painted in red. The entire store was white, except for the doors and trim, which were red. The walls were shelved with hundreds of boxes of candies, from chocolates to lemon drops to chewy taffy, all with the "Sweet Serendipity" logo embroidered on the outside. *"Can't Take My Eyes Off of You"* by Frankie Valli and the Four Seasons piped gently through the speakers. Nice touch.

I walked inside and was immediately enveloped in the aroma of this marvelous shop. It brought me back to the days of running to the corner store to buy Now & Laters and Bazooka bubble gum packs. My favorite thing to do, after eating a pack of Now & Laters, was to run up to my mother and stick out my tongue, and ask her to tell me the flavor of candy that I had eaten. Afterwards I'd be hyper for hours because of the sugar rush, and sometimes my mother would join me in eating a piece and stick her tongue at me as well. This was a throwback to my finer moments as a little girl, and all I could do was smile.

"I must thank Crystal for suggesting this place," I thought.

A voice from behind me said: "Hello Alma, and welcome to our humble shop. What can I tempt your tummy with this fine afternoon?"

It was a gray-haired gentleman wearing a white apron and hat that said "Sweet Serendipity" on the front, matching the sign above the store outside. I was taken in by his wide smile and deep, soul-searching eyes and got the impression he was the kind of person who had many stories to tell. Despite the hair, he had a youthful demeanor and appeared laidback. He reminded me of my grandfather.

"Hi. Actually I'm just trying to take a look around and see what you have here. I love what you've done with the store. Years ago it used to be a video game arcade and juice bar."

"That's what I've heard. Plenty of people here told me it was quite a popular place."

I was about to answer when it suddenly registered that he called me by name.

"Excuse me for asking, but how did you know my first name? I don't believe we've met before."

"Oh, I'm sorry," the man said, extending his hand. "I'm Mr. C, and my wife and I own this shop. Crystal was the one who told me that you'd probably stop by sometime today. Sweet young girl she is. Glad to hear she's engaged."

"Yeah, she's very lucky. She's looking forward to it and I can't blame her."

The man chuckled, turning slightly red from his laughter, his cheeks matching the red trim inside the store.

"She said that he was wonderful a few hundred times earlier when she bought her chocolates. She does seem to be deeply in love, and she's right – he's a wonderful guy."

"Have you met him before?" I asked, taking a seat on the red stool in front of the counter.

"Yep, sure did. As a matter of fact they met one another right here in the store about four months ago. They shared a chocolate sundae with sprinkles and two cherries, staring into each other's eyes for hours. They've even talked to me and the missus about getting married here."

"You can do that?" I asked.

"It would be my pleasure to do so. We'll even provide you with a special box of chocolates to take with you on your honeymoon. Oh, before I forget, be sure to take one of these."

Mr. C pointed to a sign on the counter that sat behind two bowls filled with tokens. One bowl was for men, the other for women. I picked one up from the women's bowl and looked at it. On one side there was an inscription of Psyche, a goddess from Greek mythology. The opposite side of the coin had a short note that said "Psyche, lover of Cupid." Right below the note was the number two. I looked again at the picture of Psyche, gently ran my thumb across the inscription and placed it into my pocket. The sign behind the bowl said: "If the number on your coin has a mate you and your mate will receive a free banana split for two, along with a box of chocolate truffles to take home with you."

That's when I thought of Crystal and how lucky she must feel now that she's getting married. This is such a special time for her, and I acted like such an ass this morning. I'll figure out a way to make it up to her.

"Ah! I see we have a customer. Welcome."

I saw a beautiful long-haired, brown-eyed older woman walk through a doorway from the rear of the store. She too was dressed as Mr. C, her hair flowing gently across her petite shoulders as she walked towards us, wiping her hands on a white towel. She matched her husband's loving smile and extended her hand, also welcoming me to their ubiquitous establishment.

"Alma, meet Mrs. P. She is my business partner, my wife and love of my life," Mr. C said, as he kissed his wife on the cheek.

Looking at them made me think of Javier. This could have been us had he not been so stupid. What was their secret? How do they do it? I really wanted to know.

"So Mrs. P, woman to woman - what is the secret to keeping your lover happy?"

She carefully thought over the question. "Recycling. No relationship can survive without it."

I was confused. I had asked a question and gotten a riddle as a response.

"I'm sorry, but I think you've lost me," I said.

Mrs. P leaned closer; her eyes seemed to glow.

"If you are going to meld different segments of your lives together, you both must move into a newfound sense of self. You must take something that's turned yellow, like an old piece of paper,

111

and breathe new life into it. You must grow from the tears and cries of an infant into the maturity and wisdom of an adult, always moving forward and accepting the fact that change is inevitable. The life you once had needs to be recycled into the life you want for the future. Recycle. Keep it new. If it isn't new, it's through."

Javier and I had fallen victim to this, continuing to do as we'd always done. We never embarked on anything adventurous together, and instead of planning ahead we only casually spoke about what we wanted. Our relationship had stagnated, and my feeling of helplessness was actually my insecurity of being alone. I realized I didn't miss Javier as much as I missed the presence of Javier in my life.

That was the difference.

"Great advice."

"Not to worry dear. I gained this wisdom, believe it or not, from his mother," she said, nodding toward her husband. "She was tough on me, but ultimately I proved myself as a worthwhile partner for her little boy."

Mrs. P turned towards her husband, gently stroking his face.

"For you - I'd give my very last breath all over again…lovingly and willingly."

"What an odd thing to say," I thought, as a handsome man walked into the shop. He was about six feet tall, with a neatly trimmed haircut, dark brown eyes and bronze colored skin. He wore a white polo shirt and khaki pants with brown shoes. And as I had earlier, he wandered throughout the store in amazement. The song *"Love Will Conquer All"* by Lionel Ritchie flowed gently from the BOSE speakers mounted in the corners of the store.

"Excuse me, but are you the ones who make those marvelous chocolate truffles? I'd love to buy a box of them if I could," he asked.

"Why certainly, but before you spend your money, why not try your luck with our tokens?" Mr. C replied. "You may win the chance to share a banana split and a box of our truffles with this lovely young lady."

The man looked at me and smiled. "I can only hope to be so lucky," he said as he reached his hand in the men's bowl.

He swirled his hand around the bowl, mixing the tokens around as if he were tossing a salad, then finally withdrew his hand. Without taking his eyes off of me he gave the token to Mrs. P, who glanced at it, then looked directly into my eyes.

112

"Number two," she said. "Mr. C - I think we owe this young lady and gentleman a banana split and a box of truffles.

"Coming right up."

The handsome man extended his hand. I reached for his, feeling warmth and strength simultaneously from his touch. I studied him from his hand to his forearm to his bulging bicep, and I couldn't help but think that I'd just met Adonis face-to-face.

"My name is Desiderio Antonio Carrero, but my friends all call me Desi," he said.

"Pleasure to meet you Desi, my name is Alma Hernandez," I said, feeling as if I were in high school all over again. "Please - sit down and lets watch Mr. C work his magic."

Mrs. P brought the banana split, two glasses of cherry coke and two long stemmed spoons for us. The banana split was the best I've ever had in my life, and it took all that I had to keep from requesting another one.

Desi asked me if I was busy tonight because he wanted to take me to dinner. I accepted his invitation. Mrs. P handed us a large box of chocolate truffles, just like the ones Crystal showed me this morning.

"Feel free to share these with anyone you choose. And remember - only *one per customer*. Those are the rules."

I laughed out loud, thinking of Crystal's specific instructions from this morning.

And as we turned to walk out of the shop I heard her say to me: "Don't forget to recycle, Alma."

"Trust me, I won't," I replied.

***

As I headed home from work, leaving Crystal behind to handle the late evening traffic, I walked over to Sweet Serendipity, and stood outside and watched Mr. C and Mrs. P host eight different couples, gradually going from table to table - making sure everyone was satisfied. As I checked my watch and was turning to leave the mall I nearly ran into Mike, the security guard, who stood staring at the store. He looked rather perplexed.

"Mike, you look like something is on your mind. What's up?" I asked.

"Well - I am a bit confused, Ms. Hernandez. First I see Crystal in that area talking to some fella for months, then you today with some guy. Now there must be at least twenty people in there, talking and chatting."

"What's so strange about that, Mike?"

"What's strange about it is there are so many people spending time wandering around an abandoned store front. No one's leased that store since Games Galore left years ago. You folks are walking and talking like someone owns the place."

I looked at the storefront and saw Mr. C and Mrs. P waving at me and immediately knew what to do.

"Mike, would you like a chocolate truffle? I guarantee you once you've finished it all your questions will be answered. But you may only have one. Only one per customer!"

Mike took the chocolate and bit into it as I walked away. Glancing over my shoulder I noticed his eyes opened wide to what had been invisible to him these past years. He could finally see! And soon he too would find the true meaning of love within the redolence of Sweet Serendipity. I had learned the importance of recycling from Cupid and Psyche, the architects of true love in the highest degree.

The proprietors of Sweet Serendipity looked deep into one another's eyes.

"They're playing your song," said Psyche.

"No my love, they're playing our song," Cupid replied. They held hands as they checked in with each patron, passing out free samples of their famous chocolate truffles, fresh out of the oven.

The Warden of Souls
By Yohann Sebastian
***

As I drove my Buick Regal into Guiding Light Cemetery just outside of Seattle, I couldn't help but feel the overwhelming sense of obligation that came with each visit. I always felt the compulsion to bring flowers and American flags for not only the members of my family, but for those whom I knew had passed on. Neighbors, teachers, friends - it didn't matter. There's something to be said about those who've moved into the afterlife, and I felt obligated to show respect for their memories. It's in my nature; that's who I am.

My back seat was covered with bunches of flowers and my passenger seat had a large box of flags. Later I'd simply take everything with me and slide them into small vases in front of each headstone. No big deal, really. I was more than happy to do such a thing, and would hope someone would do it for me after I pass away.

I have always felt a special connection with the dead. I know it makes no sense whatsoever, but I can't help it. Walking through the many acres of the cemetery allows me to reflect upon the stories and contributions that each person made to this life we all are trying to live. Without each one, the world might be that much different, and like it or not, we've needed them to be here with us. Some people affected my life directly; most others I never knew, but I felt that somehow, without everyone having lived, my world would not exist today as I knew it, for I believed we all have our roles to play in the game of life.

As I drove around the entrance I passed the marble statue of Callistus I, known in history as the Patron Saint of Cemetery Workers. The statue stood proudly with its hands outstretched in front of a circular pond with a small fountain in its center. The grounds were neatly maintained and appealing to the eye. I didn't need a map to find my way around, for I knew this cemetery like the back of my hand, and within minutes I was in the general area where my family laid in rest.

I put the car in park when I heard voices coming from the radio. I tried to shut it off, when I realized the radio was never on, but still I could hear whispering, which got noticeably louder then suddenly stopped.

"Weird."

I got out of my car and grabbed a handful of flowers from the back seat, placing them neatly on the grass. I emptied the passenger seat of the flags and carried everything to my family's group of headstones a short distance away.

This was always the toughest part of coming here; seeing the four headstones of my immediate family. The first stone was for my father, Clay Samuel Reinhardt, Sr., who died seven years ago in September of '98 after a long bout with lung cancer. I remember as a child how my mother constantly worked him over about his smoking habit, begging him to quit. It wasn't totally his fault, in my opinion. Dad became addicted to cigarettes while he was fighting in the Korean War back in the fifties. The soldiers did what they had to in order to relax, and smoking was definitely one of those things. The unfortunate side effect of smoking cigarettes was his premature death.

The second headstone was for my mother, Ada Clarice Reinhardt. She died six years ago from complications with emphysema, which was strange because she never smoked a day in her life. The doctor thought initially it was because my father was a smoker, but later we found the clothing factory where my mother worked for thirty years had asbestos in the walls. The combination of the two proved fatal, and she died within six months of her diagnosis. She was a good mother, too good to die in such fashion.

The third headstone was for my brother Rich, who died last year in Iraq. He was a sergeant in the Marine Corps, and was killed by insurgents while stationed in Fallujah. I remember the day I got the call that he was gone; it was devastating. My kid brother, whom I watched grow into a man, was dead at the age of thirty-eight. He followed his passion for military duty and served our country honorably, as did many other men and women in uniform. It's sad that the man who sent him to die did not act as noble when he started this war in the first place.

The last headstone was for my sister Veronica, or 'little Ronnie', as we called her. She was involved in a fatal traffic accident about six months ago while heading home from work. Both she and the other driver were killed instantly, and by far this was the hardest on me because it was totally unexpected. At least with my parents and my brother I prepared myself for the possibility that they might not make it, but for her to die the way she did was difficult for me to handle. I still have nightmares imagining the last moments of her life, and all I could hope for was her death was quick; that she didn't suffer. From the autopsy results the doctors believe she never knew what hit her. I certainly hoped that was true.

As I looked over each stone once more, a feeling of resentment came over me, coursing through my veins like a poisonous snake bite. I was so angry with God for letting this happen. I'm all that's left of the Reinhardt family. I have other distant relatives, but there's no one that I speak to on a regular basis. Of the three of us siblings, my sister was the only one who had a child. My niece Audrey lives in San Diego, and sadly enough, I hardly know her. These headstones, along with a collection of memories, were all I had left of the people that meant everything to me. Now I'm all alone.

I sat on the grassy knoll and faced each stone individually, professing my love and pouring out my inner soul. Somehow I felt guilty for their passing. I never gave these wonderful people their due when they were still alive, and as a result I have no way of making it up to them. Even though they'd never say so, as a son and brother I'd let them down.

I turned slowly to the fifth stone, which was to be mine when I'm gone. I've already paid for the engraving of the stone, and the only thing missing was the date of my passing. I'm the only one left and I didn't plan on cashing in my chips just yet, for somewhere deep within my being I knew I was here for a reason. My life had been spared the fate of my siblings and parents so I could assume something greater. I've been waiting for a long time for that "something," and was hoping it would manifest itself sometime soon. I'm no spring chicken, being in my mid-fifties.

I grabbed a handkerchief from my back pocket and dried my eyes, taking a glance at my stone a second time, when I saw something that surprised me. Thinking I'd made a mistake I rubbed my eyes again, but it was still there plain as day, slowly scaring the hell out of me:

Clay Samuel Reinhardt, Jr.
Born March 3, 1950 - Died September 24, 2005
"The Lord is My Shepherd"

My hands shook like leaves blowing in a heavy wind. The headstone reminded me of today's date: Friday, September 23rd, 2005. According to this, I'm supposed to die tomorrow.

"That's ridiculous," I thought. I took a second look: September 24th, 2005. What kind of cruel joke was someone trying to play on me? Why could anyone do something so vile? So...

"Claaaay..." Startled, I looked to my left, but saw no one.

"Claaaay......Claay........Clay.......Claaay." From all around me I heard the whispering of my name. I tried to cover my ears, but the sounds only became louder and more demanding. This continued until I heard another voice, one much scarier than the ones around me. "Clay! They're calling for you Clay! They want you here!"

I spotted something to my right. It was a figure in a black robe with a hood. The stranger was roughly two hundred feet away from me under a large weeping willow. The robe covered his face and drooped lazily over his hands and feet making it impossible to distinguish any of his features. The Voice came from this stranger, whoever they were, but I had yet to determine whether they meant me any harm.

My heart sank as the figure walked slowly towards me, its body crimping in a twisted, unnatural fashion. I still couldn't see the face or hands of the figure, but its appearance was scary enough to make me not want to stick around. The whispering of my name continued, becoming more agitated than before.

The figure was closing in fast, still moving in a contorted manner that reminded me of Samara Morgan, the evil little girl from "The Ring" when she climbed out of her watery tomb towards her next victim.

The voices followed after me as I jumped into my vehicle, my hands trembled as I repeatedly attempted to put the key into the ignition. Finally, on the third try, I was able to start my vehicle. Just as I took off a huge fog suddenly covered the road and seeped in through the vents of my car. It coiled around into the air until it inescapably filled my lungs. I passed out just shortly after wondering if this was the smell of death.

118

Seconds later I snapped awake and found myself heading straight toward the doors of a mausoleum that had been built into the side of a steep hill. Standing in front of the mausoleum was the hooded stranger, waiting patiently for my arrival.

I slammed on the brakes. The car lurched back and forth until everything came to a sudden stop. The stranger hadn't moved, despite the Regal coming straight at him, his arms at his sides and head down; the dust from the ground swirled around and enveloped him like a magician about to disappear in a cloud of smoke. For a second I didn't know what to do, until suddenly the stranger made his way to my car. I threw the Regal into reverse, turned around and sped off quicker than a NASCAR driver.

I zoomed away from the stranger and headed toward the cemetery entrance. As I saw the gate I thanked God that I was going to make it. The voices continued calling my name, mourning louder than ever, when I blacked out again. When I woke up my head was on the steering wheel. I was back in front of the mausoleum and the hooded phantasm was in front of me once more. The hood still hid the face of my nemesis, but he raised a sickly looking finger and pointed it at me.

"You cannot escape Mr. Reinhardt! The people of this cemetery request your presence!"

Before I could attempt another escape I came face to face with a crowd of people. They gathered around me and successfully blocked the car from moving. Men, women and children stood silently, their dark, sullen eyes trained directly on me. It wasn't until after I got out of the car that I realized the screaming voices had finally ceased. All of them were now smiling.

"What is going on here?" I wondered aloud. "Who are all these people?"

"They are the residents of Guiding Light Cemetery; the souls of people who have passed on to the afterlife, Mr. Reinhardt. Nothing more, nothing less," a voice from behind said.

I saw the stranger without his hood, his features now visible. I looked into the sparkling brown eyes of an older man who appeared to be in his late sixties. His thinning gray hair and beard were neatly trimmed, and he appeared quite pleasant despite the fact he scared me nearly half to death.

The man extended his hand to shake mine. An onyx was on his ring finger, but his hand appeared healthy instead of the skin and bones I'd witnessed before. I shook it gently.

119

"It's a pleasure to finally meet you, Mr. Reinhardt. My name is Angus - Angus Grimm. I know - the name sounds like I'm meant for this kind of work, but trust me - I'm a pretty swell fellow once you get to know me better."

Angus laughed at his own joke, but I still looked confused. Who is this Angus character and what the hell did he and all these "souls" want with me?

"Mr. Grimm, I appreciate your kindness, but what's this all about?"

Angus turned towards the mausoleum and pointed at something etched in stone over it's circular opening.

"I've been told that you are a former Latin scholar, Mr. Reinhardt. Look at that inscription and tell me what it says. Take your time; I know it's been a while."

As I came closer to the mausoleum I could better make out what was written, squinting my eyes against the late afternoon sunlight coming from the hill's summit behind the entrance.

"Custus Animorum."

During my high school and college years I fervently ensconced myself in my Latin studies. Since I wanted to practice law my father thought it would be good for me to learn it on the side. I saw the benefit in learning a classic language and believed it would help me become an effective attorney. Both of us were right. I've been a trial lawyer for over twenty-five years and have won more cases than Perry Mason, but without my Latin experience I doubt I would've been as successful as I've been. There's something to be said about having a firm grasp of vocabulary.

I turned back to Angus with my answer: "The Warden of Souls?"

"That's right, Mr. Reinhardt. The Warden of Souls. They were right, you haven't lost your touch."

"They? Who are they?"

"Why not see for yourself."

Angus gestured over his shoulder at the beaming faces of my parents and siblings standing in front of the crowd. They were dressed as they were buried; my father with his favorite suit, my mom with the dress dad bought for her on their 25th anniversary, my brother in full military dress and my sister with her navy blue blazer and matching skirt. My father stepped forward, arms extended, and waited for me to approach him. For the last seven years I had dreamed of holding him again someday, and our embrace was as warm and tender as ever. The same applied for all my family members, and I showed my love for each of them individually in similar fashion.

"Son, we're so proud of all you've accomplished with your life, but the honor that Angus is about to bestow on you is the most important thing you will ever do. I hope you take it as serious as I believe you will."

"What honor is he referring to, Angus?"

He placed his hands on my shoulders.

"You have been chosen by the people of this cemetery to be the next Warden of Guiding Light. You see, in every cemetery around the world a decedent is nominated by their peers to watch over the integrity of those who've been laid to rest. As Wardens, we are spiritual descendants of Callistus the First who make sure the lives of those who've passed on are remembered as their loved ones would want them to be. If humanity forgets their loved ones they are bound to repeat old mistakes in future generations. Too much focus is made on individual gain in today's world, and the sanctity of passing on customs and traditions has been lost in translation over the years. However, in keeping the memories of these beautiful people that you see before you alive, that hope for the next generation remains."

Angus paused briefly; his soft brown eyes full of love and compassion.

"You, Mr. Reinhardt, have been chosen to continue our legacy. You show respect for those who came before you, and cherish the memories of your loved ones. They have taken the love you have for them and shared that with the rest of us. In return, we are giving that love back to you with this honor."

"But the date on my headstone......I am to die tomorrow?"

"Yes, Mr. Reinhardt. At midnight you will pass away peacefully in your sleep. But before you do, we wanted to extend this voluntary honor to you. A Warden serves his community for a period of twenty-five years. If a suitable replacement has not been found by the end of that period, the current Warden stays until the community deems a successor. You were actually chosen five years ago after the passing of your parents, but at their insistence I waited until your sister died to anoint you to this illustrious position, but a Warden must choose on his own free will to take on this important task. If you refuse I will remain until someone else has been decided upon."

I looked at Angus, then to the faces of my family and the people around them. I thought again of the importance of these

people in my life. Never before had I felt so loved and needed.
How could I pass on such an honor? I knew what I must do.

"I accept."

One by one, each of the residents of Guiding Light came and
embraced me. From children to women and men, partners, lovers
and friends - one and all thanked me for taking on this important
duty, then walked away, gradually disappearing from sight. The last
to go were my family members - first "little Ronnie," then Rich and
my mother. My father was the last to hug me, and said once again
how much he loved me. Then he too disappeared.

"And now - my time has finally come," Angus said. "Please
Mr. Reinhardt, come with me."

Angus and I walked into the mausoleum entrance. I could
hear my footsteps 'clack' against the cool marble floors, the sound
reverberating off the walls. Lining the main corridor of the
mausoleum were the spirits of twelve men and women in long,
flowing white garments whom I surmised were previous Wardens of
Guiding Light coming to welcome Angus home, and congratulate me
as the newest member to the family.

"Now I will be laid to rest, Mr. Reinhardt. Remember what I
have told you. I'm sure you will be just fine."

Angus lied down in a casket that had been rolled out into the
corridor in front of an open tomb. After climbing in, Angus reached
for the black Onyx and removed it from his finger and handed it to
me.

"Keep this on at all times and be sure to give it to the next
person worthy of service. Remember - it is our tradition."

I took the ring and placed it on my finger, my clothing
changed to the black robe that Angus wore. His was replaced by a
beautiful white silk garment; his entire body glowed like an angel.

"Goodbye Mr. Reinhardt."

"Goodbye, Angus." He closed his eyes and with one final
breath, he passed on.

And at midnight, on Saturday September 24, 2005, I passed
on as well, and willingly began my new duties as Warden of Guiding
Light Cemetery.

I am the Warden of Souls.

About Detective Al

Learn more about Detective Al at his "Official" website: www.detectivealgreen.com.

Coming soon from the Detective Al Green Series:

Mystery, Malevolence & Murder – Collected Stories: Volume Two
Falling Down: Ubiquity

David T. Boyd was born and raised in Chicago, Illinois, but now lives in Brooklyn, New York. Mystery, Malevolence & Murder: Volume One is his second release (Volume Two of the series is near completion). Mr. Boyd graduated from St. Ignatius College Preparatory in Chicago, received his Bachelor of Arts in English from SUNY Empire State College and is completing his MFA in Creative Writing at The City College of New York. Besides writing, David loves to exercise, discuss politics and tell everyone why Chicago is the center of the universe. Be sure to visit his website - www.davidtboyd.com.

www.ingramcontent.com/pod-product-compliance
Lightning Source LLC
Chambersburg PA
CBHW020249150626
46552CB00020B/731